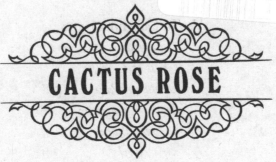

CACTUS ROSE

SAMANTHA HARTE

DIVERSIONBOOKS

Also by Samantha Harte

Summersea

Kiss of Gold

Autumn Blaze

Snows of Craggmoor

Vanity Blade

Angel

Timberhill

Sweet Whispers

Hurricane Sweep

Diversion Books
A Division of Diversion Publishing Corp.
443 Park Avenue South, Suite 1008
New York, New York 10016
www.DiversionBooks.com

For more information, email info@diversionbooks.com

First Diversion Books edition August 2015.
Print ISBN: 978-1-62681-825-5
eBook ISBN: 978-1-62681-824-8

For David

With special thanks to Abby Saul for all she has done,
Browne & Miller for their support, and Diversion Books
for making this novel such a lovely addition to my work.

One

Diablo Rock, Arizona Territory
1871

Rosie Saladay drove her rickety buckboard wagon into town like a woman gone mad. Tawny dust billowed in furious clouds as she reined in front of Diablo Rock's finest saloon, a crumbling adobe structure with a leaning porch shaded by a thatch of mesquite branches.

The day had dawned bright and warm with the promise of nothing but heat and more heat. Now the wind-swept plaza echoed with the rattling thunder of her buckboard's wheels. The reaching cottonwoods trembled in the haze.

Grabbing her hammer as she climbed down to the rubble-strewn ground, Rosie drew up her badly dyed black skirts to free her feet. At noon the plaza was nearly deserted. Adobe buildings lined the wide rutted street like drunken companions. Two dusty-looking men craned their necks to peer at her from the shade of a brushy porch awning in front of the assay office across the way. A gangling clerk wearing dark sleeve garters came out of the stone bank. He shielded his eyes and stared.

Wind caught the streaked black veil covering Rosie's face, whipping it backward like a flag. *Widow*, it seemed to signal. The widow's back.

Rosie held tight to the paper she had lettered before leaving her place earlier that morning. There was still time to forget this crazy idea, she told herself. She'd had ten teeth-jarring miles to think, but what good did thinking do? What choice did she have? It was this or lose everything Abner had worked years for.

Holding an extra nail between her lips, she hammered her message to the saloon's porch post, a pine trunk as dry as her heart. The nail sunk in like a single tooth. She smoothed the paper flat and looked at what she had written—big block letters as crude as if they had been drawn by a child. *Better drive in the second nail. No use having the paper tear off and blow away in the wind.*

Satisfied, she threw the hammer into the back of the buckboard, which was piled high with painstakingly woven grass baskets. She marched between the swinging bat-wing doors into the sultry gloom of the saloon. Her shoe heels sounded like gunshots against the warped wooden floorboards. The place was just as Abner described it. The mirror behind the bar had cracked in three places. The bar itself had a substantial layer of dust already. She seized a round-backed chair, dragged it close, and seated herself at the nearest table where she could watch the doorway.

She felt giddy and slightly sick with anticipation. Decent women didn't enter saloons, but this was where men came. She needed a man, so this was the place to find one. *Reckless,* she thought. *Crazy.* Well, if she had lost her mind, so be it. She wouldn't sell Abner's land.

The saloon was empty except for a man seated under the stairs, in the farthest corner behind her. She twisted around to glare at him. She didn't care to be watched. He had his chair tipped back against the wall. His dark western style hat covered his face. Oh, he wasn't watching her. He was sleeping. His boots were crossed at the ankles and propped precariously on the edge of the table. No spurs. No holes in the soles. He didn't stir. Couldn't he just get up and leave?

Hung-over gambler, she concluded, dismissing him from her thoughts.

The head of a longhorn steer mounted on the wall near the dozing man stared down at her with bulging glass eyes. With a shudder, Rosie turned back to resume her wait. Maybe she needed a sip of whiskey to calm herself. She wondered if whiskey tasted as bad as Abner always claimed.

She wished she could slow her drumming heart. Her surging blood made it impossible to think. With her teeth set, she watched the eye-stinging sunlight above and below the bat-wing doors. What if no one came in? What if no one wanted—?

Before she could begin to worry in earnest, two shadows blotted the sunlight pouring through the doorway. Rosie held her breath. Hope and dread mixed together in her belly. *I shouldn't have come!*

The men standing on the saloon's porch were reading her note, her sign, her... her whatever it was. Her advertisement.

She felt her cheeks flame with a wild fear that one of them would laugh. That everyone would laugh. Quickly she pushed back her black veil, adjusted her old bonnet, and smoothed her hair. Her hands were shaking. She hated that she'd had to dye her clothes. They had turned out so badly. The sleeves of her calico shirtwaist still showed tiny blue flowers beneath the thin black vegetable dye. Her blackened skirt just looked dirty.

A man pushed his way into the saloon.

Her heart leapt. She shrank back a little.

He dragged off his hat. "Afternoon, Miz Saladay," he said, chin-whiskers bobbing with each word.

"Afternoon, Mr. Rowley," she said in a voice smaller than she liked.

Her body felt like it had turned to stone. Not him. He wouldn't do. How would she tell him no? He worked at the livery stable and smelled of manure.

"I read that there notice you jes' nailed up outside there. You serious?"

"Dead serious," Rosie bit out. "You interested?" That was not what she meant to say, she thought. She was not that desperate.

He shook his head and backed away. "Now—uh, no, ma'am. Jes' curious is all."

Another man, poorly dressed, ambled in behind Mr. Rowley and looked at her, squinty-eyed. "Don't appear you're offering much," the second man said. Then he spat into the nearest cuspidor. "How many acres you got?"

"One acre turned. Pumpkins, gourds. No corn or wheat. Yet. Don't worry about that. There's plenty of work. I'll provide meals. I can dress and roast a deer if you hunt one down. I bake bread, pickle beets, turn a fine hem, patch shirts, and set a broken finger if need be," she said.

It sounded like bragging, she thought, or pleading. Not bargaining. Would this man do? She didn't recognize him. She didn't like his looks. The toes of his boots were nearly broken across.

"What kind of work can you do, Mister...?"

Shaking his head, he backed away, too. "Wouldn't catch me living outside town with rattlers and Apaches crawling behind every rock."

She felt relieved.

Behind Rosie came the sound of chair legs hitting the floor hard. Her dealings had apparently awakened the gambler. Good. He could be on his way. She would feel better. It was hard enough, doing this crazy thing in front of townsmen she had been acquainted with over the years. It was very nearly impossible to do in front of a stranger.

She realized four men had come in and were standing at the bar, looking her over in her unbecoming widow's weeds. She saw speculation in their smirks, casual insolence in their slouching bodies. It was horrible, putting herself in this position. She should have let herself die out there, alone, instead of putting herself through this humiliation. She wanted to get up and stalk out as fast as she had come in, but she couldn't make herself move. She had set this in motion. She needed a man. She had to follow through. Abner's land depended on it.

She dismissed the slouching man with the beard. Abner used to tell her about him.

"Good afternoon, Mr. Spears," she said in her most businesslike tone—at least she hoped she sounded businesslike. "You can go back to your drinking. I need a man who will work."

Ocie Spears' expression sagged and soured. "That ain't all you need, Miz Rosie," he muttered.

"It's Mrs. Saladay to you, Mr. Spears. Don't make me shoot you for insulting me," she snapped. "I meant no offense."

Ocie turned away. He said to the nearest man, "You can have 'er." Then he called to the barkeep who was just entering from the back room. "Gi'me a whiskey!"

A hard rock miner in threadbare overalls came forward. His hands had been battered by years of bone-crushing toil. He had trouble meeting her eyes. When he did meet her eyes, it was as if he knew she would send him on his way, too. He looked played out.

"Sorry," she said more gently to him. "I need someone younger."

She sensed the movement of the gambler behind her as he rose to his feet. The hair prickled on the back of her neck. He must think her pathetically desperate. Well, she guessed she was desperate. What was the use in hiding it?

She heard his footsteps closing in, strong, purposeful footsteps in long strides. Not staggering. He walked by her without a glance and pushed his way past the gathering men at the doorway. As he went outside into the sunshine she let her breath out slowly. She felt let down, somehow.

Good, she thought even so. *Forget about him. Good riddance.* She watched the bat-wing doors swinging. He was gone.

Then she noticed the storekeeper, Milt Brummit, watching her from within the crowd gathering at the door. Her stomach tightened. When had he come in?

He looked aghast at her. His eyes showed disbelief. His wiry brown beard was as unattractive and unkempt as ever. Abner used to call him Bear Brummit. Abner had a nickname for just about everybody. Bear—Milt—had always been a difficult man to deal with, always stingy in his bartering, always suspicious and argumentative. Hard calculating eyes. The story was his wife left him. Anyway, she disappeared from town one day. Nobody dared to question it. Even Milt's sons left town the moment they were old enough. He was a man bitter as bile. Nobody liked him, and neither did she.

To ignore him, Rosie turned her eyes to scan the sunburned, weathered faces gawking at her from around the room. There were perhaps fifteen men now, sizing her up like prospective buyers at an auction.

This is the craziest thing I've ever done. She didn't see a single man who would do. What had she expected? She began to lose hope.

Don't come near me, Milt, she thought. She didn't know how she would turn him away. He was a widower more eligible to marry her than anyone in town. Who would buy her baskets if she rejected him in front of all these men? She'd starve for sure.

Outside in the blazing morning sunlight, Del Grant took off his hat. Longing for a hot bath and a shave, he scratched his stubbled jaw. What was that young widow up to in there? Was she trying to hire a ranch hand? Kind of a strange way to go about it. He was glad he didn't need the work. He was no cowboy.

He saw a half dozen townsmen gathered around a piece of paper nailed to the porch post.

"Hers?" he asked, nodding toward the paper. He sauntered closer.

Several men turned suspicious eyes toward him, a stranger in town. They all nodded yes.

> *Husband wanted.*
> *Apply inside.*
> *Must be decent, honest, hardworking,*
> *and good with a gun.*
> *No conjugal rights.*

Oh, really? Del thought with a slight chuckle. Husband wanted? No conjugal rights? He poked the nearest man who was starting toward the saloon's doorway. He looked like a smithy's apprentice.

"What's conjugal mean?" Del asked, wondering if any of the men knew.

The apprentice shook his head and shrugged bashfully. "Buried her husband no more 'n a week ago. Found him dead out there somewheres, folks say. She's gone plumb crazy, I say. She knows there ain't a man in town that'll have her. Excepting maybe Milt there. He been a widower long enough he'd take on any kind of female what eats cactus three times a day."

Eating cactus... what did that mean? That she was the prickly sort, kind of sharp-tongued and not fit to live with?

Del heard murmurs and snickers all around from men who were twitching with curiosity to see the crazy widow lady sitting inside. He leaned in closer and whispered, "It means no boots under her bed."

The brawny apprentice frowned.

Del nodded his head. "That's what it means. No husbandly rights."

Looking surprised, then faintly disillusioned, the apprentice began whispering to the miners, clerks, and teamsters waiting to crowd into the saloon. One by one the men looked back at Del and then to each other. In moments they all ambled away as if remembering important appointments elsewhere.

"Too many hours in the sun, that one," one man said, glancing back at the saloon's doorway where the widow was visible inside. "Crazy as a twice-dead gopher."

"I don't care if there is gold out there," another said. "I'm not tying in with that."

So, she was protecting a gold claim, Del thought. She would need more than a husband to stay safe in this country. He felt a little worried about her, though, a widow alone, a pretty young thing in ugly dyed black clothes at the mercy of every pitfall a raw-boned scarcely settled territory could throw at a human person.

When Del pushed back through the swinging doors, the widow still sat at her table. The saloon had emptied. There was the unmistakable air of despair around her.

She lifted her eyes to him. Sky blue eyes.

"What did you say to them all?" she asked, her cheeks red, her expression stricken.

He felt more than sorry for her suddenly. Had he cost her a husband? She had a nice face, he thought, considering it was framed in so much black veil that she looked half dead. Those big eyes. Fine bone structure to the face. Beautifully shaped mouth. Why did she feel she had to hire a husband anyway? Didn't she have any pride? Out west there were ten men to every woman. Twenty, sometimes. A hundred in some places. Just to see that soft brown hair of hers would strike ardor in the heart of any man who saw her. In a little town like this, there had probably been a dozen men wanting her even when she was married. Why not go up to Tucson for a better selection? What kind of woman did a thing like this?

Del leaned against the bar.

Don't get caught up, he reminded himself. He had a job to do.

At the barkeep's inquiring glance, Del shook his head. The last thing he needed was to start drinking at noon. His eyeballs ached. His stomach felt sour. He'd had enough skull varnish the night before to last him a month. He didn't know what had come over him. He never did when he got the itch to drink. When he hit a new town with a month's pay in his pocket, always intending to head east, he always went off his feed. He'd promise himself, just one whiskey. Then he'd spy the nearest card game. Spendthrift, his father always said of him. Drunkard. Wastrel.

Yep, Del thought, his mood darkening as he tried to wipe those tired old thoughts from his mind. *I am all that, and more.*

"I saw your sign out there," he said to the widow. "Can anybody apply?"

He watched those pretty lips tighten. Her cheeks got redder. Those big blue eyes stared at him. Something like heat lightning went through his veins.

She was lots prettier than he had first thought. Parched-looking and unhappy, maybe, but the curve of her cheek was still attractive. The desert hadn't claimed that yet. And the way she held her chin out. He admired that. She had courage. He squirmed and shifted to the other foot.

Women had looked him over in the past, he thought, but never quite like that. He didn't look that bad, did he? He wished he hadn't come inside. He had business to attend to. Newfound money to spend. A job to do.

But he didn't move.

He took off his hat and studied it. It was still relatively clean. Not much rain to stain it in this country. Good quality hat maker. Nice braided leather band. Tooled silver concho in front. One of his favorites.

Then he pinned the widow with an expression that had scared off more than a few troublemakers in the past five years. He saw her shrink back. He saw the barely noticeable tremor at the corner of her mouth. *She isn't so tough*, he thought, softening inside toward her. *Poor thing. Alone there.* He understood being alone.

"Whoever you pick, does he get to inherit your place if you keel over in the hot sun some afternoon?" he asked in that same challenging tone. "No?"

She was shaking her head, frightened but steadfast.

"So, let me see if I understand you right. No conjugal rights. No inheritance. There must be some kind of payment for an honest day's work. Yes?"

"Uh, yes. Payment." Her eyes were as wide as the sky. She looked uncertain.

Del's lips tightened over his teeth. She didn't have any money. At least not the kind he was used to.

She was probably destitute. She was so darned desperate she was hiring herself a husband as her very last hope of survival. He watched her watch him. He felt like a hawk watching a trembling ground squirrel, and then suddenly, horribly, understanding washed through him like acid.

Oh, damn! He realized who she was. *Oh, this is bad. This is really bad.*

The widow.

He assumed she would be old.

He straightened. He was about to leave, fast, straight out, like a gunshot. Get the hell away quick before—

As if by conjuring, a gentleman in a fancy grey shirt strode into the saloon and stood while his eyes adjusted to the gloom. He wore a flat black hat, pearl handled pistols on both hips and polished black knee-boots. He didn't remove his hat or the toothpick stabbing out from the corner of his mouth.

Del felt his own face harden to granite. He kept his eyes steady, his lips relaxed. He could feel his cheeks flatten, his jaw tighten. He forced his breathing to slow. Ace-high straight cool. That was him. He recalled the man. He had played poker with him all the night before. Lost every dollar to him, but he couldn't bring the man's name to mind. He might not have exchanged names, he supposed. No, he had gotten the man's name all right. He just couldn't remember at the moment.

Del cursed himself. *Damn fool. Damn fool!*

Del didn't begrudge the man his lost money. He had been drunk. It was what he deserved. No, it had long been Del's way to gamble away his pay. He didn't much care. It was everything else he was suddenly remembering about the man that brought him to fighting stance.

The man looked straight through Del as if they were strangers. Then the man gave the widow a cocky sneer punctuated with that toothpick in a way that was dripping peach-ripe with mockery. Del didn't like it. He didn't like it one damn bit.

That man had no reason to look at her like that. No reason and no right at all. Del didn't like the way the man moved, either, like a mountain cat on the prowl, like he already owned the widow and everything about her. She was helpless before a professional gambler.

Del clamped his teeth together against an onslaught of unwelcome rage. It was rage he had lived with all his life. Some people were born to be gifted with plenty and ease, like that one. Some, like himself, settled for something altogether different because that's all that was left over. It wasn't fair, and damned if he hadn't fallen in with that bastard the night before all the same. Now he was tangled up in something he needed to know more about. Except there wasn't time to find out more. This was some kind of crazy showdown he had to play out without knowing the stakes.

At that moment Del wished he was standing anywhere but there. He wanted to be outside, riding away, penniless again, in need of another job, settling like always for something less than what he wanted. But safe in it. Apart.

But now, there sat the widow with her chin out, the pretty widow, alone and trembling, grief still fresh on her ashen cheeks. She was in trouble. Already Del felt the need to protect her. He realized who she was, but to help her, he had to stand there and wait and watch… looking as casual and as disinterested as possible. There was no time to think of a better way. He would have to explain later. Explain to himself. He sure couldn't make sense of it now.

"My offer still stands, Mrs. Saladay," the man said.

He stood over the widow with unperturbed assurance, his glittering gambler's eyes low-lidded, the toothpick twitching between his lips like he was chewing it.

"Every rock, every stick, every cactus. Your stock, that mud shack your husband called a house, the falling-to-pieces buckboard, even that ugly dress you're wearing. I'll buy it all. Real generous offer, too, if I say so myself. You remember, don't you? At the funeral. I gave you a week to think it over. And now, here you are. One week later. Sell to me today and you can go back where you come from in style. You can tell everybody that you sold one of the biggest gold strikes ever to be found in Arizona Territory. You won't have any takers for a hired-husband here, I can tell you that much. Give it up, Rosie. Take down that ridiculous sign out there. I'll be waiting for you at the bank. We'll have the bill of sale drawn up, witnessed, signed all legal and proper. Say yes!"

She just looked at him.

Del marveled to see a woman stand up to a predator like that. For a ground squirrel, she hadn't twitched a whisker.

Abruptly, the man strode out as insolently as he had entered. As he passed Del, he clicked his teeth from the corner of his mouth.

Seething, Del fingered his holster.

The widow looked up at Del, her blue eyes blazing suddenly with fear.

Del wasn't liking any of this. It was coming at him too fast. He felt ambushed. There was no time to think. All he could do was react. He had hired on to do a job, but now this woman needed his protection. He didn't believe there was another man in town capable of protecting her in just the way he could.

"No inheritance," he said rather harshly, wanting to sound gentler. "No conjugal rights. Why would any man agree to marry you under such circumstances?" Del sounded more critical than he intended, but if there was any chance of scaring her out of this idea, he had to try it. "Why not just hire a ranch hand?"

"It has to be a husband," she said in a small voice. "A woman can't live alone on a place with a man, a hired man, without there being talk. At least, I can't."

"Sell, and be on your way, then. Sounds like you have a good offer." *Why wouldn't she sell?* he wondered.

He was met with silence. The anxiety in her eyes fell away. He watched strength overtake the expression of terror on her face. It was beautiful! He admired her for it. He wished he possessed strength like that.

"Never," she said through her teeth. "My husband died on that land."

Ah, the dedicated, loyal widow, Del thought, wanting to believe that was all it was that kept him standing there in front of her, looking at her with this crazy idea hanging between them.

So, she didn't intend to sell out to the professional gambler in polished knee-boots who thought he saw a sure-thing in buying a widow's holdings—probably for a pittance. Del could see that she didn't want any prospective husband she had seen in here so far. She intended to stay on her land somehow, married to whoever she could talk into working for her, virtually for free. Why that was so important to her, Del didn't know. There must be a lot of gold out there. The joke might be that the land could be worthless, the gold mine empty as the widow's bed. Didn't she have a friend in this entire bleached out, drying up town? Wasn't anybody going to help her?

"How soon do you intend to make your selection?" he asked, looking around at the empty saloon that echoed with their voices. He hadn't even had breakfast yet. Why couldn't he just let her be? This wasn't his problem.

Yes, it was his problem, he reminded himself. It was exactly and precisely his problem.

"Today," she said. "We'll get married this afternoon. I need to get back. I can't leave the place with no one to watch over it."

"Valuable land?" he asked, although he was certain he knew the answer. *Today?* She really was crazy! Not even a how-do? Just an I-do?

"It was valuable to my late husband. Want the job?"

She had her chin out. Her blue eyes flashed. Her face was tanned. That meant she worked hard in the sun. She looked hungry. And tired. Widowed a week and desperate for a man to help her protect what little she had. How could he consider such a fool notion?

Nothing had stopped him from gambling away his pay the night before, he reminded himself, or drinking himself into a tangled mess. Why balk at this new development?

Del couldn't reply to her just yet. Reason was trying frantically to prevail. He felt rushed. He hated feeling rushed. Every time in the past when he made some hasty, reckless decision in the heat of emotion, he lived to regret it a long, long time. This wasn't what he had expected to be doing this day. He thought he would have more time. To plan. To do things carefully. To get everything right. It was always like that. He never learned.

Back away, now!

At his hesitation, she began to frown. She almost looked as if she was thinking of giving up when a new thought dawned. Her eyes grew sly.

"You don't mean to tell me *you're* interested. You. A gambler," she said.

"Not a gambler, ma'am," Del replied quickly, slightly offended. He didn't gamble all the time. Just when he had money. He smiled a little. "Gunfighter. I might be interested. I got nothing better to do."

What was he saying? She was talking marriage! It might not be real marriage to her, but it was still marriage.

"Are you good with that gun, Mister…?"

"Grant," he said. "Delmar Grant. Friends call me Del."

"Got many friends?" she asked.

He paused. "Actually, no, but I'm good enough with this gun that I haven't starved yet. And I'm still alive. Why do you need a man good with a gun? Apaches bothering you out at your place?" He was no Indian-fighter.

She stood up. She seemed a little unsteady on her feet. She was smaller than he had first thought, lean and rangy. He kind of admired her thin, sharp shoulders. She was probably working herself to death. He almost offered her his elbow until he caught himself.

Think twice, Del! Slow down!

She'd likely drive a man like a plow horse.

Bad idea, Del! Back off!

She reached up to find the edges of her mourning veil and straightened it. Before bringing it neatly down over her face, she pinned Del with a devastating blue glare. She looked just plain and pure loco in the head.

"My late husband got along with the Apaches, Mr. Grant. They didn't bother him. They don't bother me. It's everybody else I'm worried about. I intend to find a husband today because I am certain somebody killed my husband. This morning I realized I will be next."

TWO

With complete disbelief, Rosie gawked at the stranger calling himself Del Grant.

He believed her when she said Abner had been killed. He was serious about helping her. He was actually thinking over her ridiculous proposition. Now that she was facing a man, a real man who might be willing to marry her, she understood how crazy she truly was. She mustn't go through with this!

He had a nice face, though, nicer than she had a right to expect. He looked healthy, strong, competent.

But a gunfighter? What was a man like that doing in Diablo Rock? He had looked agreeable enough when she was assuming he was a gambler, but now that she knew he earned his living with his gun... well, that's what she needed, wasn't it? That professional gambler, Wesley Morris, he was proving to be a very persistent, frightening man. She scarcely knew the man and yet at Abner's funeral he had offered a thousand dollars for Abner's land. Why so little?

If Wesley Morris thought he was going to bully her off the land that Abner had worked for ten years, he was the crazy one. A thousand dollars? That was a mere hundred dollars per year. Ridiculous. She might be ignorant and stubborn, but she wasn't stupid.

But how was she supposed to best a man like Wesley Morris? He had come to town five years before, talking big that someday Arizona Territory would be producing gold same as California and Colorado and everyplace else he could care to name. Everybody assumed there was gold on Abner's land, too. There had to be. Why else would he spend so many years there? She had to discourage Mr. Morris and everybody else from bothering her. Mr. Grant looked like her only hope.

She watched Mr. Grant as he worked his mouth. It looked as if he couldn't think without making silly faces. Maybe he was counting his teeth with his tongue. Maybe he was just playing her for a fool.

He needed a shave, she noticed. His shirt and pants were rumpled and trail dusty, but they were quality. He had a way of standing there like he knew exactly what he was going to do. He just hadn't talked himself into it yet.

Marry a stranger, she thought. A complete and total stranger? Could she really do it? Well, she had done it before, she thought. She could do it again. It was for propriety's sake anyway. It wasn't as if it would be a real marriage. Not like she had hoped for with Abner. She would be safe in the house again. Mr. Grant would be confined to the barn. She would tell him what to fix around the place, and he'd fix it. Mr. Morris wouldn't be able to run her off, she thought, not if she had a real gunfighter on her side.

And, she could still say no. She could still turn Mr. Grant away… she could still look for somebody else…

But who?

She watched Mr. Grant straighten. He had trouble meeting her eyes momentarily but his expression had relaxed. He had dazzling, crystal-blue eyes. She liked the merry-looking creases on the sides of his face. They would deepen if he ever smiled. He had decided. Oh, it was nice what agreeableness did to the lines of his face. There was kindness hidden beneath all that stubble.

Rosie's heart leapt into her throat. He was going to help her. She was saved!

"So," he said, looking her over quickly and then letting his surprisingly casual gaze settle on her face as if he liked what he was looking at. "Where to from here?"

"The courthouse," Rosie said, her voice hoarse suddenly. She tried to swallow but couldn't. She felt more afraid than she had expected to. "This way, Mr. Grant. And thank you." She stuck out her hand.

He looked at her hand a moment and then seemed to realize she expected a handshake to seal the deal between them.

Blinking behind the protection of her black veil, Rosie wondered suddenly if Mr. Grant really understood this was not going to be a real marriage. Of course he understood! No conjugal rights. She had written it on the advertisement. He had repeated those words. He understood, didn't he? He understood the word? She meant it! Her outstretched hand began to tremble visibly.

When he clasped her hand in his strong dry fingers and gave it a single firm shake, she felt something startling, like a charge of awareness flooding her entire body in an instant. It felt like the time she saw her first scorpion, only a whole lot better than that. For a second she couldn't think. She couldn't remember why she was shaking hands with a handsome stranger.

Then he released her hand and touched the brim of his dark wide-brimmed hat with the flashing silver concho center front on the braided band. He nodded toward the door. It was time to go. It almost felt as if he were taking charge of the situation. She couldn't have that!

She moved ahead of him, painfully aware of herself suddenly as a slight woman in an ugly black bonnet, heading for her wedding at the courthouse. Her marriage to Abner Saladay had been just as inauspicious. Back then, the courthouse had been a weather-stained tent.

This was just a business arrangement, she reminded herself. But, as she stepped outside onto the saloon's porch, even in the dappled shade afforded by the tangle of mesquite branches overhead, she could hardly see for the glare. Mr. Grant moved in close behind her, crowding her almost, until she blinked and could see well enough to take a step. Her heart was racing so fast she couldn't breathe.

Was she afraid… or excited?

Rosie scarcely noticed men poised ever so casually all around the plaza. Peddlers with donkey carts up from Sonora, a freighter next to his huge wagon, a clerk in shirtsleeves on an errand, they were all watching her from the corners of their eyes. They were acting as if nothing unusual was happening that day.

As she moved along the uneven ground and across a rough plank walkway in front of the many slouching adobe stores, she could feel their eyes following her. Mr. Grant trailed behind like a dutiful employee. That was better. He wouldn't hurt her, she reassured herself. She wouldn't let him. The weight of Abner' pistol dragged against her thigh where it hung inside the pocket of her skirt. She would be all right now. Nobody would come along and kill her.

She noticed that the cottonwood trees seemed taller than she remembered. The desert wind stirred their reaching branches. The plaza felt more confining. The fronts of the adobe stores looked bright in the glaring sunlight. Her footsteps sounded loud and brisk and too fast. She slowed. There was no hurry. She was safe now. He was going to protect her.

She glanced back again. Mr. Grant was looking away, his hat brim so low she couldn't see much of his face except his bunched up lips. He was thinking. Oh no, he was having second thoughts. Well, so was she! A crazy woman could have second thoughts, couldn't she?

The courthouse was a newly constructed plank structure of rip-sawn pine shipped down from Tucson the year before. It looked like a store. It had been built when Diablo Rock was prospering, when hopes had been running high that gold would be found thereabouts. She stepped inside where it was as dim and dusty as the saloon. A clerk seated at a desk to the side was writing something in a big ledger.

He looked up, surprised.

"Is Judge Craig in?" Rosie asked, realizing suddenly that the judge might be gone. His judicial circuit throughout the county left him little time to stay in any one town for more than a few days.

The clerk gawked at her. She couldn't remember if she

had seen him at the saloon earlier or not. He might not know what she was doing there.

"We're here to be married," Rosie said.

If the judge had already passed through town, she thought, she would be forced to take Mr. Grant to the mission and ask the priest to perform the ceremony. She didn't want that. It felt less like a real marriage if the judge did it.

"He's next door at the restaurant, having lunch," the clerk said, looking intense with curiosity.

"We'll wait," Rosie said.

Oh, she was barking orders like Abner used to do. Bring in more water. Don't burn the frijoles. She must remember herself. She might be poor, and she might be nobody, but she could still behave like a lady.

The clerk knocked back his chair and sprinted outside.

Rosie turned away from Mr. Grant. Shame began overtaking her. Another stranger.

It was hard to see through her black veil. It was even harder to think. Was this really her only option? Maybe she had just been so terribly afraid that morning because of the dream.... In the dream she had been the one she found lying dead in the box canyon, not Abner. She had been running from the image all morning. Sometimes it felt like she had been dying since the very day she arrived in Arizona Territory.

When the judge lumbered in, napkin still tucked in his collarless shirt, his bearded face blossomed with a huge grin. Rosie did not particularly appreciate his good humor. She felt embarrassed.

"Well, what have we here, Miz Saladay?" he boomed. "Getting married again? So soon after the funeral? Are you sure about this?"

The man's pale eyes swept over her in her ugly widow's weeds. Then he looked at Mr. Grant. His bushy eyebrows went up with interest.

Rosie watched Mr. Grant remove his hat with casual grace. Mr. Grant stuck out his wide, steady hand, shook hands with the judge firmly, and introduced himself. He seemed perfectly relaxed, as if he married widows every day.

"How-do, Mr. Grant. Well now, come right in here, the both of you. Ah, Henry," the judge barked to the clerk. "Run next door and see if Miz Gonzales can come away from her cook stove long enough to act as another witness. Her tamales are the best in Arizona Territory. I want you to know, Rosie, that I came away from a mess of them just now to see if you were serious about this marrying business." The judge led the way into a small plank-walled room in back that served as the town's courtroom. It smelled of varnish. "Smallest courtroom in the territory," he said, directing his remarks to Mr. Grant. "Pack twelve men in here, plus me, two lawyers, and a defendant, and we're pretty much in each other's laps. Stand over there."

Mr. Grant moved to a spot near a table and twelve mismatched chairs.

"You stand next to him," Judge Craig said to Rosie.

Rosie felt every bit as nervous as she had when marrying Abner Saladay. She had known Abner about as long. Maybe an hour longer. It was hard to realize she was doing it again, marrying another man she knew nothing about except that she needed him. Strangely, she felt like crying. She looked at the judge through her black veil, hoping he wouldn't notice her tear-filled eyes.

"You want to take off that bonnet, Rosie?" the judge asked. He scowled at her in a kindly way. "Did either of you think to bring a ring?"

"I've never worn a wedding ring," Rosie said softly. "No use starting now."

The judge nodded. "Suit yourself."

She fumbled for the hatpin holding her bonnet to her hair. When she pulled it out and tugged off the bonnet, her soft brown hair tumbled free of its knot, which had been hastily twisted earlier that day. It seemed like ages ago. Rosie felt her hair cascade down her back.

"Sorry," she muttered, squirming self-consciously. "I was driving fast this morning. Must've lost a few pins."

The judge's eyes regarded her almost pityingly.

Rosie's heart felt pinched and full of hurt, but she didn't want to be killed.

"Anything you want to say first?" the judge asked. He looked hard at Rosie. "You don't have to rush into anything, you know. Wesley Morris can't force you to sell. Nobody can. He's all talk. If anything happened to you, Rosie, he'd be the first I'd speak to." He began frowning mightily.

"I think Mrs. Saladay would like to avoid any unfortunate accidents that the court might have to investigate," Mr. Grant said in a gently sarcastic tone. "I'll be seeing to her safety from now on, proper-like, so nobody can gossip about her living alone with a ranch hand who might be thinking of taking advantage."

Shocked to hear Mr. Grant state her fears outright like that, Rosie wondered if Mr. Grant was going to prove difficult to manage after all. She plunged her hand deep into her right hand pocket. Her pistol offered small comfort.

"I just think we might as well make it clear what's going on," Mr. Grant added without smiling. "Your husband's dead. As far as I can see, nobody's doing anything about his death, or protecting you. So I want it clear what *I'm* doing. I'm going to help at the ranch as best I can. She's going to… what was it you said? Pickle beets and set broken fingers?" A twinkle crept into his eyes. He flexed his fingers.

He was teasing a little, but Rosie blushed to the roots of her hair. She wanted to slap him! Didn't he understand how awful this felt?

If the clerk and the cook from the restaurant next door hadn't crowded in behind them at that moment, she might have stalked out. But this was what she had set out that morning to do, and now it felt as if it were too late. She had to go through with it. When might she ever find another man like this to help her?

Wesley Morris was waiting for her at the bank, she thought, assuming he was going to pick up a gold mine for next to nothing. That self-important, overconfident bully… he thought he could scare her into selling out… She wanted to show him he couldn't intimidate destitute widows. Gold mine. Ha! If they only knew… They were all such fools. A whole town full of them. Delmar Grant didn't even know her, but he was willing to take her side against all of them.

"Very well then," Judge Craig said, blustering like a prairie chicken. "I haven't married very many, so I'll just confess I don't remember the vows exact. I spoke them a long time back myself, and they've proven a burden, I can tell you. So I'll just say, far as I know, there's no reason these two shouldn't get married. I saw Abner buried last week, so I know you ain't married anymore, Rosie. It was a real shame, too. I'm real sorry. I'm sure Abner was a fine husband to you, not a very friendly man, but hard-working. I have to assume you're not married, Mr. Grant."

"No," Mr. Grant said with a wry smile.

"So, do you, Rosie Saladay, take Mr. Delmar Grant here as your lawfully wedded husband? Obey him and all that?" He chuckled as if he knew Rosie would never obey anybody. "For better and worse? Don't look so scared, Rosie. I'll be in town for a few more days… in case you change your mind and want a dee-vorce."

"I will," Rosie said in a diminutive voice.

She felt small and young suddenly, frightened and lost. The judge's efforts to make light of the situation only made her feel more uneasy. It hadn't occurred to her that Mr. Grant might be married. What else hadn't she thought of to ask about in her haste to find protection from Wesley Morris and all the others?

"And you, Delmar? Do you take Rosie to be your lawfully wedded wife, to honor her and protect her until death do you part, which, around here, might be sooner than you expect?"

The judge peered into Mr. Grant's face as if trying to read his mind.

It was clear Mr. Grant hadn't considered that, by marrying her, he was placing himself in the same danger her husband had been in for quite some time. Rosie had never dreamed anyone would go so far as to murder Abner to get his land, but there had been no doubt in her mind when she found Abner, lying there in the dirt, dead more than a day. Abner had been killed. Now Mr. Grant was in danger of his life, too.

"I will," Mr. Grant said.

"All right then." The judge looked pleased with himself. "I pronounce you man and wife. Kiss the bride, Delmar. This might be your only chance." He winked. It was clear he expected they would be back before the day was over.

Rosie looked up into Mr. Grant's face, uncertain how she should be feeling. She couldn't seem to feel anything. She wasn't even sure she felt safe or relieved any longer. A whole new range of possible dangers awaited her. Was he going to kiss her? Would she let him? He might be nice to kiss. Well, once, anyway.

Mr. Grant extended his hand, and, with a slight sinking of her heart, Rosie took it and gave it a firm shake.

"Thank you, Mr. Grant."

"You probably should start calling me Del," he said, "Mrs. Grant."

• • •

The so-called wagon road Rosie followed south out of Diablo Rock was a long one. It skirted looming boulders. The parched land sported the occasional saguaro cactus standing tall, with raised arms like a sentry. As Del rode on horseback alongside Rosie's buckboard, he found the saguaros unsettling. He was worried he was going to draw on one by mistake and make a fool of himself.

Ahead in the tawny sand, he could see Rosie's buckboard's tracks from earlier that morning. She had been fishtailing all over the ruts, driving like the devil was chasing her. Now that he was with her, was she really any more safe?

"How far?" he asked, finding himself tempted to tease

her and call her Mrs. Grant again. The sound of it made him nervous. *Wife. Mrs. Delmar Grant.* If she had been scared crazy that morning, he was scared crazy now, too. *Married,* he thought. All for a few dollars.

"About ten miles," she said.

She had put her black bonnet back on to protect her hair from the sun and the dust, she explained. It made things easier for him, Del realized. Covered like that, she still looked like that crazy hard-bitten stranger he had confronted in the saloon. It was easier to think of this as a job, just another job, for money.

But there had been a moment, standing in front of that judge, with the witnesses squeezed in behind them, when he had studied Rosie Saladay's drawn face and felt a tug of something more than pity. More than protectiveness. He'd seen a frightened human being behind those sky blue eyes. He felt moved to tenderness and compassion. She was placing herself into his hands for safekeeping. It was an unexpected responsibility. If something happened to her, it would be on his head.

What would Mr. Wesley Morris do now, Del wondered. Just like that, he remembered the man's name. Wesley Morris. Professional gambler, speculator, and probably even a mining expert on occasion. Cocky s.o.b., too, used to getting whatever he wanted. What did a man like that want with Rosie's hardscrabble land?

What was out there that was so important Rosie would marry a stranger to protect it? Del saw nothing in the surrounding arid countryside to indicate there might be major gold deposits nearby. He had been in the gold country of the Colorado Rockies. This land looked nothing like that.

Rosie kept glancing over her shoulder.

"What are you watching for?" he asked when he noticed she kept craning her neck as if expecting something… or someone.

"I'm doing what you should be doing, Mr. Grant," she snapped.

Had she been weeping? he wondered. Her eyes seemed red.

"I'm keeping an eye out for my husband's killer coming along to finish the job. With me dead, the land is up for grabs."

She sounded tough, but Del wasn't fooled any longer. She was petrified.

He slowed his horse. He twisted around in the saddle and searched the road behind them with wind-dried eyes. He hadn't eaten yet that day. He felt hollow and irritable. Looking back, he hadn't realized they had been climbing. No wonder her horses' pace was so slow. The town appeared small and forlorn, back there among the rocks.

He saw nothing on the horizon but a few scattered shacks and farms, sparse sage brush, big jumbles of boulders, and cactus of every possible description. The high desert held a strange beauty different from everything he had seen in the West so far. He saw nothing on the dusty track but Rosie's wheel marks. There were birds. A lot of little birds. The sudden movement of a jackrabbit startled him. He felt the sun's heat on his back, burning his shoulders through his shirt and searing the backs of his hands. There was the clean scent of sunbaked earth. The cottonwoods thinned just outside town. Here the honey-colored soil was nearly bare. Ahead was more brush, more rock, more damned saguaros.

There had to be water where she lived, he thought.

He heeled his horse to catch up to her. Water in itself was valuable. She had a crate of supplies in the back of her buckboard now, and fodder for her horses. The supplies replaced a lot of delicately woven baskets she had had when she arrived in town. He wondered where she got them. She had traded them at Brummit's General Store after the wedding ceremony while he picked up his horse at the livery barn. He bought a whole box of ammunition, too. Big display of strength, he had thought, carrying the box in plain sight across the plaza. Defending the widow, he had announced with his purposeful stride. His bravado had disguised his deeper amazement that he had just gotten married. He had joined Rosie at the buckboard as if they'd been man and wife for years instead of minutes.

As far as Del knew, that Wesley Morris was still waiting for Rosie to come crawling to him at the bank. He had to smile over that. She was a brave one. He had to give her that. Any other widow would have sold out and driven straight through town for Tucson and a stagecoach to an easier life.

"Where were you headed when you stopped at that saloon last night?" his new wife asked as she drove the buckboard wagon into suffocating open-aired heat. She drooped with fatigue over the reins. She was probably talking to keep herself awake.

But Del's hair rose on the back of his neck. Could she read his mind? Did she have any idea how he felt, tying up with her? He couldn't be sure himself. It was somewhere between foolish and being suspended on tenterhooks.

"How did you know I was at the saloon last night?" he asked, immediately on guard.

"You were there this morning when I walked in," she

said. "That means you were there all night, too drunk to walk, and without any money for a room with a bed."

"Sounds like you know all about men and saloons," he bit out, feeling tense and sober suddenly. He didn't appreciate her assumption. "Was your late husband a drinker?"

"Abner? He had a nip now and then when he went to town, but he went to town so seldom it was never a problem. Abner was a good man. He worked hard. If I hadn't come into town this morning, where would you be headed now?"

She wasn't easily distracted, Del noticed.

"My last job ended in Mexico," he said. "I was coming up from Sonora, headed for Tucson and the stage line there."

"A stage line to where?" she asked, pointing as they approached a barely perceptible fork in the wagon track ahead. "That way. In between those big rocks."

He saw the morning's wheel marks cutting deep at the turn. She had almost overturned there. It was a wonder she didn't kill the horses, driving that fast.

"I was heading back east. Home."

Well, that was true, wasn't it, he thought. He was always heading home. He just never arrived. Gambling away his money always saw to that.

She made the turn slowly and drove on until they were well within the cover and shade of towering boulders two hundred feet high. Formidable fortress walls, Del thought, looking up at the rugged beauty. In one spot the buckboard barely made it through.

After a few hundred feet, Rosie reined in and took a long pull from a canteen she had tucked beneath the seat. She offered him some of the water. He rode in close to take the canteen from her. Her eyes were dull with exhaustion now. She glanced at him, almost as if she were afraid to admit to herself what she had done, and she quickly turned her eyes away. She was taking an awful chance, he thought, bringing a stranger here where anything might happen. Who would protect her if he turned out to be a bad man?

"How long has it been since you were home, Mr. Grant?" she asked.

"You won't call me Del?"

She shook her head.

The ugly black bonnet wobbled on her mass of soft brown hair that had been hastily knotted back up and tucked in place with the hat pin. He remembered the sensation he felt seeing her long hair tumble free. For an instant she had been like a different woman. He had found her astonishingly attractive.

"Since the end of the war," he finally answered. His tone was carefully devoid of emotion.

"I see," she said. "If we hurry, we'll be there in another hour. My horses are tired. They're old, these poor girls. I've tried saving up to buy a new horse or two but there's hardly enough for beans and sugar. You may not like it out here, Mr. Grant."

"It'll do," he said. So long as she didn't pry into his past. That's where he drew the line.

As long as there was to be no conjugal associations between them, Del thought, he didn't feel too guilty about marrying her. This wasn't going to work out between them anyway, this crazy arrangement, he thought. Just looking at her distressed expression he knew it, but being married would do for a while. He'd see her safe before heading east again. And before he left, he would come clean. He owed her that.

They went on in silence, her driving with less anxiety in her posture, but now it was him looking around at the looming walls of bisque-colored stone that lined the road. It proved to be a natural pass and a steady climb opening into a cozy desert valley. There had to be quite a lot of water here, Del thought. He saw patches of green everywhere. Cedar, juniper, mesquite trees, and an occasional cottonwood. A lot of tall grama grass. This was a higher elevation where Indians summered, not as hot as the desert floor, and isolated from troublemakers. He'd find antelope and black-tailed deer on the ridges, he was sure. He liked the place right off.

The wagon track was barely a trace there, a mere hint of a trail over rough gravel and deep sand, yucca cactus and scrubby bushes now and then. Nothing to graze cattle, he noted. No mineral deposits that he could see. But then he was no expert.

And yet there was something about the place that held his attention. It had a haunting beauty. This was the land Rosie's late husband found. This was the land for which she had joined herself to a stranger in order to defend it. This was the land a gambler in polished black knee boots wanted to buy with his self-importance and his intimidation. Del felt intrigued. It felt as if the little valley was as alive as an old woman, possessing great dignity.

Maybe all Wesley Morris wanted was Rosie Saladay herself. Rosie Grant, he corrected himself.

Was that all it was? A middle-aged man after a pretty young woman? Did Rosie fail to realize every man in Diablo Rock had wanted her that morning? He had seen their faces. He knew what he saw. She might appear a bit dried up and desolate at the moment, but he would bet she cleaned up real sweet. She was like the blossom on a prickly pear cactus, a rose of unexpected radiance and delicacy in a desert otherwise as lonely as death.

Del smiled to himself.

That sounded downright poetic, he thought. He had better stay the hell away from his Mrs. Grant. It might prove more difficult than he expected to keep his head clear about the withholding of those celebrated conjugal rights.

"There," she called out, slowing again to point ahead. "The ranch house."

"Ranch?" he asked. "Looks like all you're raising here is cactus."

"That's what Abner always called it, the ranch house. It's a shack, Mr. Grant. Plain and simple. You'll be sorry you took up with me with so few questions asked."

"Are you sorry yet?" he asked.

"Not sorry. Guilty, maybe. I won't have any pay for you... for a long time."

"Figured as much," he muttered to himself. Luckily it wasn't a problem at the moment. They had no need of money here. "You seem awfully dedicated to your shack and cactus farm," he said in a lighter tone.

She turned to gape at him and a smile suddenly tugged at the corner of her mouth. It was the first time he had detected humor on that thin face. It warmed him to see it.

"It's the only home I can remember, Mr. Grant."

Her only home? That was puzzling. Hadn't she lived in a house as a child? He didn't press with further questions. There were plenty of days ahead to fill in all the details of her past. His concern was with what he would tell her, and how much.

Del decided to ride ahead. He had followed her dust like a homeless puppy long enough. He heeled his horse and galloped ahead. Now he looked around to judge the lay of the land. Where might he expect to spot claim jumpers approaching? Where might he find the best defensive positions? He would need to know what had happened to her husband if he was going to defend her... and this place.

Goddamn, the house was ugly!

The foundation was local flagstone piled in layers in what he hoped were lines wide enough to support walls and a floor... was there a floor?

He reined at the door to wait for her.

The walls of an addition were covered with a collection of sun-bleached boards and what looked like kindling. The main part of the house was adobe that was crumbling off to reveal rocks, planks, and mud-bricks. The house was decorated amusingly with a store-bought pine door set in a frame along with a big nine-light window intended for a larger building, like a hotel. Both were set in crooked.

There were closely set pine log beams sticking out all along the roofline. The beams must've been hauled from distant mountains. The roof itself reminded him of a mounded apple pie made from tan gravel. A dirt roof. Oh, just what he wanted to live under. It wasn't even a sod roof like he had seen on the prairie. It was dirt. A huge heavy pile of it. Luckily, it was not the rainy season. He screwed up his face and sighed. Now he was certain he was crazy. *Welcome home, Delmar.*

The nearby barn's roof was constructed of the same mesh of mesquite branches they used to make all those porch awnings in town. He dismounted as Rosie drove the buckboard in close by the side of the house. Strolling across the sunbaked yard, Del looked up at the barn roof. It must've taken months to collect that much brush, climb that branch-built ladder over there, and pile the brush thick enough to keep out the sun.

She had a bag of cornmeal in her arms as she came up to him and squinted into the sun that was about to sink beyond the western ridge.

She grinned. "So, what do you think?"

The effect of a full smile on that young face was just as Del had anticipated. Her face was transformed. He gazed at her for a long moment and thought, *I am married to this woman.* The word conjugal crossed his mind and had to be quickly discarded.

Del grinned back. "I'd say this is just about the most pitiful excuse for a human habitation as I have ever seen. I can see why you'd stake your life to hold onto it."

Oh, that had not come out quite as he had intended.

Her grin wilted.

He clamped his teeth together. The last thing she needed was somebody making fun of what she valued, he reminded himself.

"It's taken a lot of work to keep these buildings from falling into piles of rubble," he said, remembering he was her hired husband, not even a friend. No need to charm her. No need to cheer her up. She didn't have to like him. If she didn't pay up, eventually he would feel not the slightest twinge of regret in leaving her to this desolate valley. That's what he told himself.

"Thank you," she said, sounding surprised that he

noticed. "I did the best I could. The barn roof was the hardest, but I just couldn't let Faithful and Old Belle stand in the hot sun day in and day out."

"You built the barn?" he asked. He was shocked a man let his wife do such work.

"Pretty much."

He didn't know what more to say.

She had said her husband was a hard worker, but the place was falling to ruin. He didn't know what kept the house standing. The place was neglected beyond belief except for charming lines of rocks marking a path to the door and around to the barn and along the corral fence.

All around came the faint whirring sound of hummingbirds flitting in close to drink from little medicine bottles hanging from the jutting roof pine-log rafters. There was a badly made stool beside the crooked front door, an attempt at a cactus garden under the window. Signs of Rosie's attempt to make this a home were everywhere. She had wind chimes made from packaging string and sticks and odd bits that clattered cheerfully in the breeze. The sound brought a smile to Del's desert-dry face and warmth to his heart.

"Was your husband lame... or sick?" he asked before he could stop himself. Or lazy, he wanted to add, wondering why she had been forced to shore up the barn's roof unassisted.

"He was always working," she replied quickly in Abner Saladay's defense. "Abner never stopped working. He would've worked all night if I had let him. I think he dreamed working, but this wasn't where he did his work."

That was plain, Del thought, without speaking. Rosie looked tired enough, trying to preserve the respected memory of her late husband.

Del swept the heavy bag of cornmeal from her arms and started for the house. Might as well survey the damage inside. Then he was going to find out just what sort of man Abner Saladay had been that a little thing like his cactus rose had to make a garden from rocks.

Del glanced back at the corral. Oh, yes. There would be no time for rest. The horses were still standing in the buckboard's traces. He had his work cut out. He'd tend to them next. He followed Rosie through the badly set store-bought doorway. Oh, good. There *was* a floor. It was made of broad, flat fieldstone. He had never seen a better floor.

"The main room here was the only room we had at first," Rosie said as she came inside and skirted a small table made of wind-twisted cedar in a surprisingly charming style. A thick pine post rose from the center of the floor to the roof rafters reassuring Del. At least there was something holding up that dirt-pie up there.

She had a small black iron cook stove, the kind that disassembled and could be mail ordered from a catalogue back when Diablo Rock had been a pebble in the middle of the trail up from old Mexico. The stovepipe likely needed cleaning. There was a dry sink stacked with a few precious pieces of china and crockery. Many were chipped. She had shelves on the walls lined with little baskets. Everything was crooked but cared for, tidy, homey-looking. He liked it at once. Curtains. Rag rugs. Would he find linens and quilts on his bed?

With dusk coming on, the big window still let in enough light to see by. But Rosie moved quickly, and perhaps a bit nervously, to strike a Lucifer match and light an oil lantern standing in the middle of the table. The sudden flood of

44

golden lantern light added a surprising feeling of welcome to the otherwise humble room. There was a deep, squat adobe fireplace in the corner. It looked old. Really old.

She watched him look around.

"Abner built this place himself on the foundation that was already here. See this floor? Stone worn down by those who lived here long ago. Took him a year, he told me."

"I didn't think this area has been settled that long," Del said, surprised by such a cool, solid place to stand.

"Not by white men, Abner told me," she said. "Mexicans, perhaps. Long ago. Indians don't stay put long enough to build houses with stone floors. Certainly not Apaches. The fireplace draws really well. I've never had any trouble with it. We were always warm here, not that it ever got very cold in winter."

She walked to the back of the room where a calico curtain hung in a doorway, also set in crooked. "This was Abner's room."

She pulled the curtain aside. Del joined her, curiously intrigued, and poked his head in. There was a narrow plank bed in the far corner, coarsely woven rugs and boldly patterned blankets covering most of the walls. The floor was packed earth with a woven grass mat beside the bed. He saw a crude wooden desk cluttered with small wooden boxes and several leather-bound field journals, rolled and tied closed with leather thongs. On an arrangement of shelves he saw thick leather-bound books and small oddly shaped objects difficult to identify in the gathering dusk. On the floor was a small open basket filled with crusty looking blue rocks he knew to be valuable to Indians.

"What's all this?" he asked, nodding toward the objects

on the shelves.

"Abner called them artifacts," she said.

She moved across the main room and stood in front of another curtain in another doorway. She didn't draw that curtain aside. "This is my room. You'll sleep in the barn. I'll make up a nice—"

"Sorry, Rosie," Del interrupted. He turned to face her. "If I'm here to protect you, I'm not going to be caught snoring in the barn when whoever you think is after you sneaks into this dirt pile of a house to kill you. I'm sleeping in here, with you."

She backed away. She shook her head vigorously.

"No, you'll sleep in Abner's room then, or we'll go right back to town and untie this ridiculous knot. Getting married seemed to make sense when I woke up this morning!" she cried. She looked around in a panic. "I just couldn't stay here alone another night—"

He hadn't meant to upset her.

"I didn't mean *that*. His room will do fine," he said calmly, resisting the urge to get closer and pat her on the shoulder or something to ease her mind.

She drew a pistol from somewhere in the side of her skirt and brandished it at him. It was an old thing. He could see that well enough in the lamplight. It was well oiled. It probably worked, and could probably do him some serious damage if she pulled the trigger. Her hands trembled badly. He had shocked her. She looked damned determined to use the gun on him, too. He had certainly underestimated her, he thought. For a ridiculous moment Del wondered if she had killed Abner herself.

"You mind yourself, do you hear?" she yelled. "I know

how to use this gun, and I won't think twice to use it on you. This is a business arrangement between us! Nothing more."

"No conjugal rights," he repeated flatly, wanting only to calm her. "I know the meaning of the word, *Mrs.* Grant. I'm always on the lookout for a good gun, though. Can I have a look?"

"No!" she snapped. "If you would, please," she added with effort, "get the horses into the barn. I'll light the fire and get supper on. It'll have to be corn bread and fat back tonight. I'm tired." She waited while he watched her, unmoving. "Just go outside. Please!"

She looked terrified of him.

To his knowledge, he had never terrified a woman before. He decided to have it out before she cocked that thing and killed him.

"So, you and your late husband didn't sleep in the same room, in the same bed," Del said.

Her eyes seared into him. Yep, he had spooked her but good.

That bed in Abner's room hardly looked big enough for a man to sleep in much less have any kind of conjugal associations with a woman. Maybe that wasn't any of his business, Del thought, but in a way it seemed like it had to be.

She still held the gun on him, but she wasn't thinking about shooting him anymore, he concluded with some relief. She was remembering, and it was not pleasant, whatever it was.

"I came west to marry Abner six years ago," she said. "He needed somebody to keep his house for him while he worked. He couldn't do it all. He was near to starving when I got here. And he said he couldn't have a woman here unless..." She licked her lips nervously.

Suddenly it all came clear to Del. An arranged marriage was all Rosie knew.

"Propriety's sake," he said for her, feeling sorry for her.

She nodded, her expression grim and sad. "He married me, but I was just his cook and housekeeper. After a while he didn't do anything around here, he was so busy. I had to do what I could." She stuck her chin out. "So I did."

"That left him free to prospect." Del thought he understood the arrangement completely.

"If you agreed to my proposition because you think there's gold in it for you, Mr. Grant, you are wrong. There's no gold. No gold mine. Got that?"

"All right," he said, growing suspicious and wary.

"Ten years ago Abner came west for his health. He walked all over New Mexico Territory—this land was part of New Mexico Territory back then. He walked and got stronger. When he found this valley he bought it."

"But not because he found gold," Del put in, still not believing there was no gold. Not that he cared about gold. He just didn't believe a man could work ten years on anything else.

"No, Abner was not a prospector. There's no gold, I promise you. Abner found something more important. He used to be a professor back east. Union College, I think he called it. He had friends back there. He used to write to them a lot. He didn't write in the last few years. He... he got so caught up in his work he didn't think of anything else. If it hadn't been for me, he would've forgotten to eat and sleep."

"Then what?" Del realized he was feeling ever so slightly angry with himself.

"He bought this land because he found a special place, an ancient place where people used to live long ago. *Long ago*, Mr. Grant. Maybe even before Apaches and Mexicans. He told me never to speak a word of it to anybody. He made me swear a vow! But I have to tell you because now he's dead. For a week I haven't known what to do. I've been crazy with grief and fear. He valued this place more than his life. I almost hate the ruins—they killed him. Now they're mine to protect. You can't tell anyone, Mr. Grant. Promise! This is a solemn vow, more solemn than what we said in front of the judge. I swear on Abner's grave, I will hold you to this promise!"

She cocked the gun.

Alarm prickled through Del's body like heat lightning. This time she was serious. The widow lady looked crazy as a twice-dead... What had that man called her? He had married a lunatic. What harm would another promise do?

"I promise," he said in a tone that had lured two men to draw on him in the past and regret it. "What kind of thing did Abner find?"

"Cliff dwellings, he called them," she said in a hushed tone of respect. "Stone houses—as big as a village. At first he stayed around the ranch house with me, doing chores, but I knew he was just helping me adjust to life here. In time he had to go to the place where he did his work. I was just an ignorant mill town girl. I never cared about his ruins that much. He gathered his specimens. They made him so excited, those tiny scraps of things. He would bring them to me. His face would glow with something I never understood. Everything was so precious to him. He worked for hours. Hours! Days! Years! It didn't matter the heat. It didn't matter if he went hungry. I don't even know what he did there. I would have to force him to lie down. Then he would sleep like the dead until he would jump up like a shot, go out at dawn without a word." She shook her head, remembering. Her lips trembled with hurt and sorrow.

"Sit down yourself, Rosie," Del said gently. He could see how distraught she was becoming. She might kill him accidently. "I promise I won't tell. Everybody in town thinks there's a gold mine here. Let them think it. So long as I'm here, they won't get close to this place."

He watched her study him as if he were a lizard on a rock and she was trying to decide if she should smash him or let him crawl away to safety. Finally she let down the hammer of her pistol and laid it on the table. Del realized he had been sweating.

She sank to a stool, trembling all over.

"When I first got here, the house was alive with scorpions," she said. "I thought I'd die! I'd come so far. I couldn't go back! I had nothing to go back to. At first I liked the quiet. Then I started to hear things. Whispers. Singing. That's when I made the wind chimes. Oh, Abner got so mad one time. I used some little piece of a thing in one of the chimes. He called it… what was the word. A shard."

Del wondered if she was going to cry now. Had she cried when she found her husband dead and realized she was completely alone in this desolate place with all these objects that meant nothing to her? It might do her good to cry except he didn't know what he would do if she did.

"Abner was twenty years older than me," Rosie went on. "At least I think it was twenty. He never told me how old he really was. Even after his lung fever cleared up, he kept his distance. He believed it was catching. He said it had claimed his whole family back east. After a while he had no money left. We went hungry. He apologized for being a poor provider. He brought pieces of baskets to show me. I got the idea to make them myself. I needed something to hold things around here. Then I made extra ones. Abner suggested I trade them for goods we needed... jerky, oats, pinto beans. Things got easier." She smiled wistfully. "I think he came to care for me," she said. "I always hoped he cared... just a little."

Del's heart went out to her. All those years here without even love to comfort her. It was heartbreaking.

"But what made you settle for a marriage like that?" he asked. "Didn't you want a family?"

She rubbed the sleeve of her badly dyed bodice. He realized it was the same fabric as that hanging in doorways.

"I thought about it at first," she said softly, as if the memory hurt more than she wanted to let on. "I hoped for more. When I was on my way here, that's what I thought would happen. When he explained there was to be no conjugal union between us, I had to accept it. All I really wanted was a home anyway. This room became my home. I helped Abner add on his room, and then we built mine. Even when he was working at his site, I felt safe knowing he was out there and he would come home to me at night. Safe enough, anyway. A person's never really safe, are they, Mr. Grant?"

"I wish you'd call me Del," he said.

"I can't do that," she said softly. "At least not yet. Maybe after I know you better." She gave a giggle and cocked her head like she knew the arrangement was ridiculous. "What about you? Where are you from? How did you come to choose gun fighting as your trade?"

He debated a few seconds and then said, "I had better see to those horses."

He went out into the dusk.

At the door, he paused. He wasn't ready to talk about himself. He might never be. He felt heat coming off the sunbaked adobe walls and saw sunlight gilding the pines on the ridge. He could see why she had become afraid, alone here, her husband dead. Where was Abner buried? He'd ask about that later. Tomorrow, maybe. He laid his hand on his holster and sniffed the air. It was surprisingly easy to smell a man in the desert. The desert itself smelled of sage and sun-warmed earth and clean dry air. Men smelled of sweat and hair oil and leather if they wore boots and gun belts.

Did he smell someone nearby?

All he smelled was a barn that needed mucking, two tired buckboard horses and his own unwashed self.

He listened to the crunch of his own footsteps as he crossed from the house to the barn. He pulled his saddlebags and bedroll from his horse. Banjo, they had told him the horse's name was back at the livery where he'd bought him months before. Banjo had proven to be a good horse.

He'd been riding Banjo ever since, sleeping in hotels when he could afford it, eating when he was lucky, heading home, he always told himself. Home. But somehow there was always a whiskey bottle to detain him, a card game to throw his money away on. Then he'd need work again. There was no shortage of work for a man with a gun and therefore home stayed far away.

Del looked back. He saw Rosie watching from the patch

of golden lamplight shining out the doorway of that so-called ranch house. It blended perfectly with the surrounding boulders. It was an ugly place, but it almost seemed alive.

Now he was having fancies.

Six years, he thought.

What a thing to settle for in a place like this. No family. No friends. No children. No hope.

That big nine-light window looked awfully bright as evening settled in. They should cover it with a blanket at night. The house would become invisible. At the moment it was like a beacon.

Rosie closed the door. He smelled the first whiffs of wood smoke lifting into the air from the stone chimney. He felt the emptiness and solitude of the valley close in. He had never felt such isolation before, not even on the road up from Sonora with banditos and Apaches lurking nearby.

He sighed. He hadn't answered her yet. What had he been doing in that saloon the night before?

What was he going to tell her?

He scratched his stubbled jaw. *When* was he going to tell her? That was the question. Whenever it was, she wasn't going to like it.

Not one damned bit.

Three

Rosie lay in her bed that night, every muscle tensed, her arms stiffly at her sides. The pistol felt cold in her hand. If she listened carefully, she could hear the soft crackling of the fire banked in the fireplace in the other room. The fire cast a comforting amber glow under the curtain that covered her doorway.

She studied the log beams overhead that supported the closely set sticks holding back the roof. The rugs and blankets covering the walls softened the ugly plank and kindling construction of the addition and helped hold in heat at night. Her traveling trunk stood in the corner, holding her few changes of clothes. She'd owned almost nothing before coming west.

She swallowed hard. Why should she feel so sad? Mr. Grant seemed trustworthy enough. He wasn't going to push aside the curtain covering her door and force himself on her. She was more than surprised at how well her rash decision of the morning had turned out. She had been lucky but once again she was bound to a man who would never join her under the covers and warm her with his hands.

In the back bedroom, Del squirmed on the low plank bed. The canvas mattress had to be stuffed with something that felt like sand. It had taken on the shape of a much smaller man. Del's lanky body didn't fit.

The blankets had a peculiar smell that reminded Del of sunbaked rocks. It wasn't a bad smell. Just unfamiliar. He would need to air them in the hot sun, and maybe beat the rock dust from everything.

And he longed for a bath. His jaw itched with a day's growth of beard. He was hungry. Rosie had fed him supper but it hadn't been enough. She had fresh supplies but she had been too tired to cook much. He was no cook, that was certain. She scarcely ate anything herself. He suspected she had been near to starving out here. The whole set-up made his jaw ache. Apaches lived more comfortably than this.

Climbing from the bed, he pushed aside the curtain covering his doorway. The bedroom needed a window. The air was stagnant. He couldn't breathe. The fire had burned low. It lent an eerie glow to the main room where the table stood with stools on either side. How lonely it felt. They had a rug over the front window now. She had her own curtained doorway closed. Not much protection for her, he mused. She was probably worrying, waiting for him to push his way in and bother her. Any other kind of man would not have been able to resist.

He grinned and breathed deep. He was resisting, that

was also certain. Did she appreciate the kind of man he was? He wondered if she would fall asleep with her pistol in hand.

Back in Abner's room, Del crouched in front of the shelf across from that so-called bed. He searched the book titles and artifacts. Academic texts. Pieces of broken pottery. Small bones. Smooth blue rocks crusted with brown. Nothing captured his attention.

He stood and rummaged through a wooden box on the desk holding letters dating back ten years. He didn't bother trying to read them. It was too dark. There were a dozen soft leather-bound journals that were rolled up, each filled to the last page. Del felt as if he were holding the sum total of Abner Saladay's life in his hands. There was a trunk in the corner holding threadbare shirts, faded long-handle underwear, much-mended socks, and a change of linens for the bed.

He didn't know what to do about his discomfort. He couldn't sleep in a dead man's bed in a dead man's room. He felt like he was in a grave. What had Abner Saladay thought about as he lay here all those years while a young woman, alive and pretty, slept close by? What did he find so fascinating in his books? How come the man hadn't wanted a family? Men suffering from lung fever took the cure in the dry air of the west and went on to marry and raise a passel of children. What had been the matter with the man?

And who had killed him?

It was no use staying awake all night, wondering. He'd ask his questions tomorrow. They might never figure it out, he and Rosie, but at least they would try to find out.

In the firelight-lit main room again, Del listened for the

sound of Rosie sleeping. The room was silent except for the fire hissing softly as it burned down. He found it startlingly difficult not to imagine Mrs. Rosie Saladay Grant lying on the other side of that thick adobe wall with that abundant brown hair spread out all over her pillow. What kind of bed did she sleep in? Was the mattress hard-packed sand molded into the shape of her body? Did her bedding smell of rocks and soil and abandoned dreams?

He lifted the stout pine branch wedged between the brackets on either side of the door. He set it aside and opened the door to step out into cold night air. It never failed to surprise him how cold it could get in the desert at night.

The valley was as featureless and dark as the inside of a pine box. Overhead, however, the sky dazzled him with stars. A new moon was rising, lending a faint blue-white glow over the barn's mesquite roof. Del moved silently to the stool that stood near the doorway. He sat wondering what it was like to live there year after year.

What would it be like to really be married, he wondered with more interest.

He had never considered marriage. In the past it had never crossed his mind. First there was the war and that utter chaos. Then he was moving west, blindly, one place, another place, nothing in between but places to sleep, places to eat, an occasional friendly woman to ease the monotony. Thinking about it like that, Del felt almost as if his life had been as empty as Rosie's. He supposed war did that to a man.

What had it been like for Rosie here, night after silent night? This was the only home she remembered? There was so much he wanted to know about her, it startled him. What was it going to be like, living here with her? How long would he be able to endure it?

Inside the house, only a few feet from where Del sat outside in the night's cold air, watching the stars, Rosie lay in bed with her heart pounding.

What was he doing out there?

She strained to hear. Wasn't he tired? Couldn't he sleep? Was he under the impression he had to guard the house? Surely no one would approach in darkness. It was almost impossible to cross the valley at night without stumbling over something sharp and hazardous.

Rosie felt surprisingly safe, knowing Mr. Grant was there. But night had never been her enemy. Daylight was. Abner had been killed in daylight. Someone had found him out at his secluded work site and ended his life in broad daylight. She fought a sudden onslaught of tears. Had Abner suffered? Had he time to think of her? She wished she could cry out her grief, but she dared not attract Mr. Grant's attention. He might come inside again. He might come to her doorway. She might... she might want him to.

She had already done her crying, anyway, alone with Abner's body lying stiff and cold in the back of the buckboard. Crying never helped anything. Wasn't that what she had always been told?

What was Mr. Grant doing out there?

Had he left her?

She sat up in bed in full panic.

"Mr. Grant?" she called out. "Are you out there?"

When she heard no reply, she called his name more loudly.

She held her breath, listening, heart thudding. Surely he wouldn't have abandoned her the very first night! She heard the door close. The heavy branch dropped into the brackets. Her breath went out in a huff of agonized relief.

"Did you call me, Rosie?" she heard his voice come softly from the main room. "Are you all right?"

"Are you?" she asked, hating herself for acting like such a ninny.

"Sorry I woke you. I was just getting some air."

• • •

"I'd like to see the cliff dwellings," Del said as Rosie led the way out of the house the following morning. It was still cold, but the sun would soon be over the eastern ridge, bringing with it the full heat of the day. "I can't imagine why a bunch of stone buildings would be of such importance to anybody that they'd kill over them."

"The spring is over this way," she said, leading him to a cluster of boulders on the far side of the barn.

Del got the impression the boulders were huddling together and turned away as if to guard their precious secret: water. He saw that the barn had been positioned to shield the location from anyone approaching from the pass. Immediately he saw how the water should be diverted to a barrel—if she had a barrel. As it was, the water dribbled from a crevice in the rock and disappeared down into more rocks, vanishing into the ground again. It was as precious a find in the desert as any gold deposit.

A tin cup stood poised on a nearby rock. She had a wooden bucket, which she placed beneath the dribble. He waited in silence while the bucket filled, ever so slowly, and then he dipped up a cup of water, which he offered first to her.

A slight smile dawned on her face. She looked a little pale as if she had not slept all night.

"Why, thank you, Mr. Grant," she said, accepting the cup and draining it.

"You're welcome, Mrs. Grant. How about it? Can we go there today? How far are they from here?" He dipped up a cup of water for himself. "These old stone buildings." The water tasted deliciously cold and refreshing.

"I don't mean to be secretive or impolite, Mr. Grant, but I simply have to know you better first. Abner—"

"I know, I know. He died there."

He twisted away. She didn't trust him. She had no reason to, he reminded himself. He understood that. She had rushed recklessly into an arrangement with a stranger no sane woman should have ever accepted. Or a sane man, for that matter. She had to have been more desperate than he could imagine. She had pulled a gun on him the night before, too. He had better remain on guard.

With the filled bucket, Rosie started back toward the house.

She should've moved herself into town, Del thought. She should've let eligible townsmen approach and court her in their own time. Didn't she know how pretty she was? Didn't she yearn for a second chance to have a real life, better than this one? When she was out of sight, Del rinsed his face and gulped down a second cupful of water. He saw no way he was going to get a bath or even a decent wipe-down from that dribble.

From what he could see, this land looked no good for anything at all. He went into the barn to feed his horse and her two old girls. The place hadn't been cleaned in weeks. Everywhere he turned he saw urgent need of repairs.

He was half done mucking the barn by the time she called him for breakfast. He smelled the coffee all the way to the spring where he did his best to scrub his hands with sand. Was he going to have to make soap, too?

• • •

Moments later Rosie watched Mr. Grant gulp her terrible black coffee and gobble cold corn bread. He must be starved. She must cook more for him. When he hadn't come in after she showed him the spring, she worried he had become angry that she refused to show him the cliff dwellings that day.

What difference did it make if he saw them?

Was she afraid to show him the ruins because he might become obsessed with them, too? Would he become like Abner and forget about her? There was a haunting, fascinating quality about the ruins that made even her appreciate them, at least for their antiquity. She had admired Abner for protecting them. He talked of looting in ancient tombs somewhere in a far-off land. *What was there to loot here?* she wondered.

Would Mr. Grant appreciate the ruins or start searching for the gold as she was certain her husband's killer was trying to find? *Was there any gold?* she always wondered. She was almost afraid there was. Had Abner kept that from her? Was Wesley Morris right? Oh, she hoped not. She so wanted to triumph over him.

"Rosie, do you have a water barrel?" Mr. Grant asked, shaking his head when he saw her shaking hers. "A small keg? Large pickle jar?" He shook his head again, teasingly. "No? You need something to hold more water. How did you live here so long, if your husband was at the ruins every day? What did you use for money? Just the basket making?"

He looked dumbfounded, and Rosie realized that the life she scratched out here seemed more than bleak to Mr. Grant. Had it been unbearable? She bore it well enough, she supposed.

"I'll make a list of things we'll need the next time we go to town," she offered. "You need a water barrel?"

"How do you wash your hair?" he finally asked. "I know you keep things clean here. I can see it."

"The wash tub," she said, indicating a small wooden tub propped in the corner.

Water in it would be ankle deep.

"Oh," she exclaimed with heat flooding her cheeks. "You'd like to wash up. I'm sorry! I've brought you to the end of nowhere—I warned you." She chuckled at the awkwardness of it. "If you want to busy yourself for a while, I can fetch and heat water for a bath. I'll wait outside while you bathe."

He started laughing and almost couldn't stop.

"I wish you could see your face, Rosie. Yes, I would appreciate being able to wash up. I saw your little truck garden out there. Does it grow much?"

She shook her head. He was laughing at her, and she felt

embarrassed. "There isn't enough time in the day to keep the plants watered. Abner suggested irrigation, but I didn't know how to do that. Even if I knew how to make troughs to carry the water, I'd need lumber... it takes hours to weave a basket to trade for things. I'd rather buy food than lumber. Mr. Brummit has warned me that soon everybody in town will have all they can use of my baskets. Then what will I do?"

"He can ship to Tucson, can't he?"

"Oh, I hadn't thought of that. I couldn't even raise chickens. Too dry... too hot. Even with a shaded shelter—"

He cut her off with a wave of his hand. "There must be some way of surviving, if people long ago lived here long enough to build stone houses."

She looked at her new husband and marveled. She'd managed to find herself another nice man, at least.

Del worked in the barn, cleaning and repairing until the late morning heat made it necessary for him to stop and rest. He spent an hour in the shade, staring at the spring, trying to imagine how he could fill a barrel, irrigate a truck garden, and build a horse trough that wouldn't go dry in the sun. The fact that Rosie had survived here six years made him wonder all over again if she had lost her mind long ago. This was no life for anybody.

She had sourdough bread just out of the three-legged kettle on the hearth waiting when he went in to eat that noon. The inside of the house was stifling. He marveled that she had endured it. She had forgotten to heat bath water, but it didn't matter. His hair was dripping wet, his shirt rinsed in the spring, wrung out and put back on, cooling him considerably. Glad to put off the chore of bathing, he slept like the dead that night, tired and full of more corn bread, completely unaware of the hard bed, its dusty smell, or the ache in his muscles.

He was up early the next morning to ride Banjo all around the valley in search of anything he might use to improve Rosie's place. He found little but kindling and patches of tall buffalo grass. Then he worked on the corral fence for a few hours and the barn roof. He greased the buckboard's axels, all the while wondering if he might be able to clear enough rock from under the spring to create a small pool. That might work better than a water barrel.

By the end of the third day he had dug what amounted to a muddy sinkhole under the spring. The dry earth soaked up water as fast as it dripped. Del's enterprise was a failure. He had a bad case of sunburn on his back and hands like those of a hard rock miner now, but he felt better than he had in years.

When he went inside at the end of that day, Rosie finally had the washtub in the middle of the floor half-filled with cold water. She poured in a kettle-full of steaming water from the cook stove. She laid out a ball of precious scented soap, an old but fresh towel, and smiled.

"Sorry it took so long to find time for this, Mr. Grant. By the time you've cleaned up, supper will be ready," she said. She had some kind of thin stew bubbling on the cook stove.

She took herself outside.

Grinning sheepishly, Del stripped off his dusty clothes and stood a moment in the middle of the stone floor wondering how a full-grown man went about getting clean in a washtub. Did he put one foot in and try to keep the dribbling water inside the tub? Or did he just stand there and get water all over the floor?

He washed his hair first, worried his fingertips over the three-day-old stubble on his face, marveling to think he'd been too busy to shave, and finally he gave up keeping things tidy when he saw the puddle he was standing in. At least he got clean. He took a fresh change of clothes from his saddlebags. After he dressed, he felt better than he had since his bender at the saloon in Diablo Rock... how long ago had it been? It felt like a year.

By the time he came back inside from emptying the washtub outside on her garden, the water on the ancient stone floor had evaporated into the dry air. There was enough warm water left in the kettle to shave.

When Rosie came inside a half hour later, she looked windblown and refreshed. She had an armload of long grass that she had just gathered. She laid it near the fire. Grass was about all there was in abundance in the valley, Del thought, that and cactus. He had been working so long he failed to notice she was nearly done weaving another large new basket. He marveled at the intricacy of it.

She was wearing a brown shirt and a denim skirt. He couldn't remember when she had changed out of her widow's weeds. It might have been days ago. His first thought was to realize she wasn't as old as he had first thought, seeing her in that saloon. She looked different, somehow. She looked... good.

"Oh, you look so much better," she said. "I was afraid you were going to work yourself to death in this heat. It's nice that you shaved. So many men in town give it up."

He shrugged. It posed no hardship to keep himself up, he thought.

"You keep busy here yourself, don't you?" he said. "You changed your clothes."

She looked pleased he noticed, he supposed.

"I saw enough grass around here you could weave for years," he said.

"I already have been." She smiled though. "Large ones…" She indicated baskets holding her dry goods beneath the dry sink. "Small ones…" They lined her shelves. "I've lost track of how many I traded at Mr. Brummit's store. I want you to know how grateful I am for all the work you've been doing. I haven't had to suggest a thing."

It was nice to be thanked, he thought. He had been glad to help her. "The ground's too dry to hold any amount of water, though," he said. "I made a mess of the spring."

"I saw that," She gave him another smile. "No matter. I've lived with it a long time."

For all her pleasantries, however, Del thought she was beginning to look uneasy. He wondered what was bothering her.

"How old are you, Rosie?" he blurted, thinking perhaps a blunt question would distract her from whatever she might be getting ready to ask him. He still wasn't ready for questions.

She blinked. "I came here when I was eighteen."

"So you're twenty-four," he stated for her. "Younger than I thought. Black wasn't your best color. I'm almost thirty."

She nodded as if she hadn't given his age the slightest consideration. He found that oddly disappointing. Apparently she wasn't seeing him as anything more than a good ranch hand. He had started noticing her as something more than an employer, that was certain.

She took her place at the table and served up the last of the stew, which they had been eating on for what seemed like forever. Same as the day before, the stew needed salt. And vegetables. And meat. He couldn't identify what was in it. He wondered if it really was cactus soup. She didn't immediately begin to eat hers.

He could feel it coming. Whatever was on her mind was standing in her eyes now, making her expression sober. He had been working so long it surely must have given her far too much time to think.

"You still haven't told me where you're from," she said.

He busied himself eating.

"Do you have any family?"

"No, no family," he lied. "No home since the war. Nothing worth mentioning."

He finished the last of his slice of sourdough. Then he met her eyes, conscious of keeping his expression as bland as possible. *Don't ask anything else, Rosie*, he said silently.

Rosie watched Mr. Grant gaze at her as if he hadn't a care in the world. Ah, that poker face, she thought. No family? No home? What about the war? Was there a man in Diablo Rock who hadn't served and made sure everybody knew on which side? Hadn't he served? A few men hadn't.

He was a gunfighter, after all. Was he hiding something? Only that afternoon she had wondered if he might be hiding out. Had she taken a killer into her house? Might he be the one who killed Abner? That was a crazy thought. Would she be dead the moment she revealed the location of the cliff dwellings? Her thoughts started to run wild.

"Are you wanted by the law, Mr. Grant?" she asked with her heart racing. "Is that why you're willing to be here with me, away from—"

Mirth made Mr. Grant's pale eyes sparkle and dance. She'd never seen a man's eyes do that. It sent a thrill through her. She felt light-headed suddenly. His face stretched into a grin that showed all his teeth and transformed his face from handsome to breathtaking. He burst into a laugh that was so infectious she started to chuckle along with him.

He leaned back from his empty bowl. She knew she wasn't filling him up, but there was nothing she could do. If he hadn't guessed already, he soon would realize that after six years she had no idea how to cook.

Mr. Grant's laughter subsided.

"No, Rosie," he said, still grinning. "I am not wanted by the law."

Four

All that night Rosie brooded about Mr. Grant. She tossed and turned, unable to stop thinking about him.

In the morning, she watched him drink his coffee. He always blew on it first. Then he tested the heat of the rim of the cup with his lips, a habit she was beginning to enjoy. She watched him eat a chunk of sourdough dipped in molasses. He took big manly bites. He glanced at her, caught her watching him, and stopped chewing. Quickly she looked away. She felt self-conscious. She wished he would say something. Glancing back, she saw him smile as if he liked being watched.

"It's good. Really. Hard and dry, just how I like it."

She tried not to laugh. She wanted to remain serious. She wasn't satisfied with his explanation of his past the night before. There was something too casual about him. He had to be holding something back. She wanted to ask again but hesitated.

Now he looked as if he had decided what to do for the

69

morning. As he moved to get up from the wobbly stool, she pinned him with a no-nonsense stare. She felt impatient suddenly. Why did she always have to be so careful with a man? She had to have it out with him. She couldn't go on lying in bed all night trying to figure out why such a man would stay with her.

"Now that you know what a terrible cook I am, do you still want to stay here and protect me?" she asked, hating the tremor in her voice.

His eyes flew to her face. *Ah, look at that,* she thought. She had surprised him. But his crystal eyes were clear. They did not seem to be harboring ulterior motives. "Why do you ask?" he asked.

"If you still want to stay, I need to know more about you."

She saw something change in his expression. She was sure of it. Yes, there it was, a flash of irritation around his eyes. A tightness to his cheeks. Then stillness settled over his face. He was every bit as much a gambler as a gunfighter, she thought, feeling a deep sense of alarm. Why, then, did he lose all his money at poker? She realized she was hardly breathing.

"You didn't need to know anything about me the day you married me," he said in a tone that was slightly challenging and quite intimidating.

Her heart leapt with apprehension. If she pressed, he might leave, Rosie warned herself. She would be alone again, for good this time, at the mercy of her fears and whoever was out there waiting. She wished she hadn't spoken. Why did she have to know? Why did she have to know today? Because...

Because she was trying not to like him so much.

"I know there's something you're not telling me, Mr.

Grant. Who are you? Where are you from? How do you know how to do all these chores if you're just a gunfighter?"

He moved his mouth again like he did when he was thinking. Counting teeth. Weighing his answer, she realized. Why should it be so difficult to answer her? If she hadn't been so scared, so determined, she would have laughed. He looked so funny. She yearned to trust him. She just didn't dare.

For a moment Mr. Grant looked away. He glanced around at the room, but Rosie supposed he wasn't really seeing the room. He was thinking, remembering, choosing his words with care.

"I grew up on a farm back east," he said in a way that made her uneasy because of the sheer casualness of it. "I… uh… left at an early age to find adventure in the west. It turned out to be a lonely life. On my last job I worked for a Texan who was buying cattle in Mexico. He needed someone to guard his strong box. He found and paid for his cattle. I didn't care to sign on for a long dusty cattle drive back to Texas. So I moved on. Because I hadn't been up this way, and hadn't seen Tucson, I decided to ride in this direction. I ran out of money in Diablo Rock. I needed another job… you came along… looking needful in your widow's weeds." He tried to brighten his expression. "I decided to stay on to help you."

He left a long pause in which Rosie tried to get herself breathing again. Why did she feel so afraid?

"I stayed on because I like helping people," he said. "Even though we're married, Rosie, we can break this off any time we feel the bargain no longer suits us. Are you feeling that way this morning? Do you feel ready to carry on

71

here by yourself now?"

"I thought you said you were heading back east to go home." Had she found the gap in his story? "Tucson is westward from Texas. Not eastward."

"There's no hurry to get home." He glanced away as if distracted by a disturbing memory. "No one's waiting for me."

Her mouth went dry. She believed him. She realized she really did. Well, she wanted to so badly. She wanted this tension that had sprung up between them to ease. She wouldn't ask again. She made a silent vow to herself.

"I've enjoyed being here these past few days, working for you, Rosie," he went on to say. "I'd like to stay on if it's all right with you. There's a lot more to be done."

Rosie relished the words. After so many years with Abner, with each year growing more and more desolate, and with so many unanswered questions still between the two of them, Mr. Grant's disclosure seemed candid. Almost refreshing. She could actually imagine life there with him, a real life, not just this awkward arrangement. Their days together might go on forever. Suddenly she didn't want to know anything more of his past if it troubled him that much to talk about it.

What if… what if something more developed between them? she wondered. Her heart blossomed with hope. It felt like the sunrise inside, and she found herself breathing easy in a way she had never known before. His expression had changed, too. He looked…

Poor man.

He looked sunburned.

· · ·

In moments Del got himself outside where he could start his day's chores. He crossed to the spring and scowled down at his fiasco. Splashing water on his face, he wondered where the water came from. Where did it go? He kicked at some rocks and sent a pile tumbling. Damn.

What was he going to do about her?

He went on with what had become his morning routine with the horses, but he was brooding now. He found it hard to complete one task before starting another. After a half hour, he paused in the increasing heat. Why not tell her everything? Right now. He liked being with her. That was just the problem. He liked it a lot. He felt himself settling in, and that was no good.

It couldn't last. This parched place wasn't where he wanted to end up. This was temporary. She'd been crazy to hire a husband, and he'd been crazy to accept. Were they meant for each other—two lonely, crazy people? He hoped not. The last thing he wanted was to crawl into this grave of a place with her and dry up. He was alive. He was very much alive.

And so was she.

She was a nice woman, he thought, as he surveyed the repairs on the corral fence. She deserved better than this, and didn't even know it.

She deserved better than him. How was he going to tell her? She wasn't stupid. She sensed he had a secret. He stripped off his sweat-soaked shirt and threw it on the ground.

Just go inside and tell her. Come clean, and clear out. That's what she deserved. Honesty. Not lies.

He went to work with his back toward the house.

• • •

From the doorway, Rosie fanned herself with her apron and watched Del wrestle with a fence post. His shoulders were so broad, gleaming with sweat and sunburn, rippling with strength. He finally got the post straight and then used a rock to pound it deeper into the ground as if he hated the thing.

He stood, panting, wiping his brow, studying the ridge, the barn, the road from the pass, the open area in front of the house, and then finally, her. He put his hand on his hip, still breathing hard, just staring at her. She realized she wasn't breathing. When he bent to retrieve his shirt from the ground, she sank to the bench by the door, her knees weak.

• • •

Rosie spent another restless night straining to hear something from the other bedroom. She relived every moment of the day, from his words about his background and his most recent work to the way he avoided her for the remainder of the day. She fed him, lunch and supper, but he spoke hardly a word more. She hated the silence.

His story hadn't been that shocking, she thought. Had she angered him by asking, by making him remember something painful? His background seemed nothing to be ashamed of or secretive about.

The next morning when he came inside from his morning visit to the spring to wash the sleep from his face, she had the kettle on. She ground the coffee beans with enthusiasm. She would make things up to him. He had been willing to help her. She must prove she was coming to trust him.

"I've decided to show you the cliff dwellings today," she said, expecting he would be surprised and pleased. As the coffee got hot, she felt excited and hopeful.

He looked at her blankly, brows raised. He drank the coffee when she poured it, but gave her no compliment as she had come to enjoy. "Is it far?" he asked.

"If we pack lunch we can stay all day and be back by nightfall."

"All right. Good," he said. He grabbed a corn pone and went out.

"I'll be ready in a few minutes," she called after him.

At the door he nodded. "Buckboard, or just the horses?"

"Just the horses."

He motioned that he understood. He didn't seem eager to see the ruins as she had expected, she thought with disappointment. Had she made too much of keeping the ruins' whereabouts secret? Was she making too much of everything?

Something must be wrong. Things had seemed so easy between them right at first. She had enjoyed that. Now he seemed wary, closed off. She realized she was starving for real conversation with him. With anyone, really.

An hour later they had Faithful packed with canteens and a few supplies. Maybe Mr. Grant had lost interest in seeing the ruins, but Rosie felt proud to share Abner's treasure with him. She watched as he saddled Old Belle and Banjo. She liked the way his hands moved as he worked, pulling hard to test the cinches, smoothing his hand on the horses' flanks, crooning to each horse softly. She felt safe, she realized, for the first time in days. Maybe... ever.

They rode out slowly, heading to the northern end of

the valley by a circuitous trail barely visible between brush and cactus. When they had nearly reached the ridge, she reined. It had been almost three weeks since she had last been in this area. Her excitement vanished and sorrow swept over her.

She felt reluctant to retrace the steps she had taken that awful day she dragged Abner's body back to the house. It was as if she was going to find him dead all over again. She couldn't go there after all. Mr. Grant would be so put out.

Dismounting, she pretended to adjust the cinch on her saddle. She heard Mr. Grant dismount, too. Her eyes burned with unexpected tears. She had thought she was ready to do this. She didn't want Mr. Grant to see her cry.

When she felt him move up close to her side, she pretended to be looking at something on the ground. He put his hand on her shoulder. She went warm all over at his touch and felt soothed and calmed. He had an unexpected kindheartedness about him she was beginning to depend on, she thought. He seemed to know when she was most afraid.

"It's all right, Rosie. No hurry. All this time I thought you didn't trust me enough to bring me here. I thought you feared I'd rob you… or something, but now I see this is difficult for you, isn't it? You're remembering the day you found your husband, aren't you?"

She struggled to speak. "I had to figure out how to get him back to town by myself," she said softly. Grief washed through her, overwhelming her. "He wouldn't have wanted me to bring anyone here to get his body. So I couldn't fetch help. I had to bring him out myself."

"I'm sorry," he said.

From the corner of her burning eyes, Rosie watched

him study the trail, squinting against the sun's glare, his cheeks tight and red from the heat. His lips looked dry.

"So, where is the stone house?" he asked. "I don't see anything."

She dashed away her tears. "I don't think I've thanked you enough for helping me, Mr. Grant," she said, finding her courage returning. "You've done more for me than you know."

He gave just the smallest twitch of a shrug, as if marrying her had been the least he could have done.

Smiling suddenly, Rosie was able to draw a deep breath. "We're not there yet. I think you'll be very surprised."

She indicated a grand tumble of granite boulders ahead, most as large as her ugly dirt house or larger. She walked up to a mass of dead pine trunks and rubble that appeared to have slid down from the ridge above. She motioned for Mr. Grant to come closer. When she moved aside some brush, she watched him squint at a small strangely shaped grey handprint on the boulder. Her heart swelled with wonder to see it again.

She watched him touch the place. He had long, nicely shaped fingers, roughened from work. He leaned in for a closer look.

She remembered the first time she saw the ancient handprint herself, proof that once long ago someone with a hand about the size of her own had laid his hand here, covered in some kind of primitive paint, and left behind a mark for all time.

"The first time Abner showed me this, he was beside himself with excitement," she said, her heart aching with the memory. "His wrinkled old face glowed. He said few people have ever made a more momentous discovery than this. And this was *his* discovery." She swept her arm to indicate the valley. "He claimed he owned a piece of mankind's history."

As she spoke, Rosie felt her late husband's pride glowing in her heart. Her cheeks went wet with tears again. She turned away. She had loved Abner in her way.

Mr. Grant traced the handprint and marveled that it seemed to be part of the stone itself. Nothing came off on his fingertips. Then he looked at her and his eyes were soft with amazement.

"I don't know what to say, Rosie," he said. "Who made this mark?"

"This way," she said, dashing away her tears. Crying in front of him didn't feel so terrible after all. He seemed to understand. She felt eager now to share the ruins with him. "From here we'll have to walk. The passage is very narrow, barely wide enough for the horses."

On foot, Rosie led the way ahead of him with Old Belle following. Del came next, helping Banjo squeeze between the boulders, and then came the packhorse. The boulders were so immense and closely set it was a miracle anyone had ever discovered the place. Every so often Del saw more handprints and markings in simple shapes, like a child's crude drawing of a lizard, jagged lines, or zigzags scraped into the rocks long ago.

Rather than feeling as if he were climbing into a grave with Rosie, Del felt as if he were walking into a dream now, moving deep into the past. He had seen otherworldly places in crystal caves back home when he was a boy, but this was far stranger.

The passage was so narrow the daylight was blocked, but after a few turns he could see dazzling sunshine ahead. In moments they had ducked beneath a low point, a rock so huge it could crush them in an instant if it hadn't been balanced on so many others.

And then... there it was.

An amazingly rugged rock-walled box canyon with no outlet beyond. Like a secluded paradise, it was decorated with tall reaching cottonwoods dotting an area a fraction of the size of the valley. To the left was the gurgle of water emerging once again from the rocks. It was likely the same water as that near Rosie's house. Beneath its thin stream was a shallow pool in the shape of a teardrop. Just what he had been trying to create back at the house, Del thought.

At the point of the teardrop, the water became a thin ribbon again that meandered some fifty feet before disappearing once again into the rugged canyon floor. All along the way were lush grasses standing still in the pouring sunlight.

There were bushes and boulders all around, and on the far side stood a sheer layered bluff of tan colored stone rising three or four hundred feet to a high wooded mesa. Del drew in his breath at the sight. He had never seen anything like it.

Within the bluff and tucked into a huge hollow beneath a slanting brow of rock fifty feet wide was a habitation he could not have guessed at. The brow of rock shielded the habitation from anyone standing directly above it on the ridge. There, nestled under the brow like a hive was what looked like a small town constructed entirely of stone.

The cliff dwellings were not stone houses standing on the valley floor as Del had expected. They were high crumbling walls with small square window openings and short doorways at one with the stone strata of the bluff. Everything was tucked into and blending with the surrounding boulders. It seemed almost as if the dwellings had grown there.

All around were more markings on the box canyon's boulders, ancient markings that Del could suddenly, inexplicably read. These lines represented a river. Here was a stalk of corn with two ears growing on it. There was a man, and a hand, and an animal with horns. He looked at Rosie in astonishment. She watched him with shining eyes.

"What do you think?" she asked softly.

"Whoever lived here should've been perfectly safe from the outside world."

But Abner Saladay hadn't been safe here, Del thought. He had died here.

"It's hard to imagine anyone living here, and yet there's proof that people did," he said.

As if cowed by their grandeur, Rosie picked her way closer. The trail seemed nearly impossible to follow. The sound of their horses' hooves echoed like time itself.

Del followed, so transfixed he almost fell over his feet. When they came upon a small clearing in the shade of the bluff, Del saw Abner's canvas lean-to lying on its side. Abner had had a field table and stool set up there. The table lay broken, apparently smashed. Had that happened during a struggle?

There were artifacts lying in the dirt. Del saw rounded stones with indentations, something that looked like a stone club with rotting binding holding the stone to a rotting wooden handle, and heaps of arrowheads. One smaller heap clearly showed finger marks in the dirt—someone had scooped up a handful.

Del's heart leapt with surprise. His attention sharpened.

There were fragments of woven baskets lying nearby, pieces of broken pottery that might have been fitted together before the struggle, something that looked like a small animal curled up, hard to the touch of his fingertips. Dead hundreds of years and found in the ruins? His imagination began to run wild. Del could almost feel Abner Saladay's fascination and raging dedication to this place.

Del wondered what story the signs here could tell him if he could only decipher them. He held up his hand for Rosie to remain silent while he studied the tracks. He didn't want to miss anything.

There was a wooden stool Abner had sat upon to write. It lay on its side. A soft leather-bound journal lay half buried in blowing sand, pages flapping. Del picked it up and saw it contained meticulous ink sketches of the markings on the rocks. On another page was a sketch of the cliff dwellings themselves, then a diagram that must be rooms Abner had explored. There was the bottle of ink overturned, a stain in the sand where the ink had spilled. Abner's quill pen had blown away and lay caught in a hillock of bunch grass.

Del looked up at the towering stone ruins again, trying to imagine how long it must have taken for the inhabitants to gather all those rocks and fit them together and then cover them with mud-mortar against the wind and cold of ages. Abner Saladay had written extensively in a small precise print to utilize every bit of his journal's pages. There wasn't time for Del to read any of it. Absently, he rolled the leather cover around the curled pages and tied the thong. He stuffed it into his shirt.

"There are more journals back at the house," Rosie said. "You probably saw them in Abner's room."

"What was he planning to do with all this information?" Del asked.

"I don't know. Who else would care about such a place except Abner?" she asked, sounding sad. "It seems all his work was for nothing now."

Del went on scanning the area, seeing that the lean-to shelter had fallen in that direction, that the table had been smashed in this particular way, that the artifacts scattered thus and so. He saw hints of boot tracks, scuffmarks… was it proof of Abner's death battle with an attacker? Had someone followed him into the box canyon and surprised him? Was there another entrance? What were Del's chances of ever finding it?

"Where was Abner's body when you found it?" Del asked.

"Over here," she said. "I sometimes came here at noon if he had gone off with no food. I would find him writing here in the shade, talking urgently to himself in a whisper. He wouldn't hear me come up. I would have to call out to him. Or he might be up there in the rocks somewhere, sketching. Sometimes he would show me something, but sometimes he was just… not of this world. He usually got home at dusk, but that last night he didn't come. I sat up waiting for him. I dared not come looking for him in the dark. He had never been away so late. I kept telling myself he had forgotten himself. I was sure he would come home in the morning, but when he hadn't come after dawn I was afraid something had happened. I hoped he had just worked too hard and decided to stay the night. I planned to scold him. I kept thinking I would meet him coming home through the passage, or on the trail, but the farther I got the more worried I felt."

Rosie stopped talking. Her lips tightened, her forehead creased. Del watched her fight to hold back fresh tears. He saw twin drag marks in the dirt where she pointed. That was where she dragged her dead husband's body, he thought. Her face had gone almost white.

"Then I saw him," she said, her voice low, "lying over there as if he had fallen down. If he had been under the lean-to, I would've thought he was sleeping. Lying there exposed like that... I knew right away he was dead," she said, her voice growing strained. "I called out to him, and then I went up to him and got down like this..."

Del watched Rosie tiptoe closer to a spot on the ground. She crouched and reached out a trembling hand. He could imagine her husband's body lying on the ground.

"He was stiff," she said. "His face..."

She stood up abruptly and wrapped her arms around herself, tight, like she was very cold.

"And you were sure he had been killed? He hadn't just died."

"He was away from everything. Not under the lean-to out of the sun where he wrote in his journal. He didn't have some kind of attack and fall off his stool. He didn't die climbing around in the ruins. He didn't stumble and hit his head on a rock. He was reaching for something. He looked... his face... he looked enraged."

"No knife wound? No gunshot wound? No blood? Nothing?" Del began to wonder if Rosie had simply been too grief-stricken to realize Abner could just die.

She shook her head. "Not that I could see. But the expression on his face. Doesn't that mean anything?"

Del didn't know what it might mean.

But maybe that was why there was nothing being done in town, Del thought. Everyone in town assumed Abner Saladay died of natural causes, just as he was doing.

"You said Abner was frail," Del went on. "He worked too hard. He didn't eat much. He didn't sleep much. He might have had a heart attack. He might have suffered a stroke and stumbled around in confusion, trying to find his way back."

Rosie looked at him, her eyes wild. She kept shaking her head. "Someone else had been here," she whispered insistently. "I felt it."

Del could imagine how terrified Rosie must have been to find her husband dead. He crouched in the gravel, looking for something he feared was not there, evidence. How was he going to convince her there had been no murder? An old man had simply worn himself out and died. That was all there was to it. It was difficult to tell if there were footprints in the dirt. The soil there was rocky. Abner might have been looking for arrowheads. He might have been over here relieving himself. He might have seen something move, a wood rat or rattler...

Straightening, Del paced beyond the spot and looked back at the fallen lean-to. He looked up at the ruins, mute and stolid. The wind blew dry and warm against his face. He took off his hat and shielded his eyes to scan the rim of the box canyon. The sky overhead was a perfect pure blue.

Was there a disturbance in the gravel over there, just beyond some small rocks where Abner might have struggled with someone? he thought. The wind had been blowing the sand around for weeks. Any tracks would have long since been obscured.

Who might have found a way into this place? Wesley Morris? Surely that fancy-shirt with his polished knee boots didn't stray far from a poker table. If Morris wanted to know what Abner Saladay was hiding, Del couldn't imagine him hiking around in the desert himself. He would hire it done.

If Abner had been surprised by a stranger, he would have defended his find. It was far more likely that Abner would've killed an intruder than to have been killed himself. Tired suddenly, Del shook his head. Anyone might have stumbled upon this place. A stranger, long gone. Abner had stumbled upon it, years before, hadn't he? What would an intruder do if Abner fought and died, trying to drive him away? Flee, of course.

"Did Abner carry a gun?" Del asked.

"No," Rosie watched him with a darkening expression.

Any minute she was going to be bristling mad again, Del thought, when she realized he was no longer convinced Abner had been murdered. After all, nothing had happened at the ranch house since Abner died. No intruder tried to get past them to sack the ruins of imagined treasure. Rosie wasn't on guard all the time anymore, either, Del thought, wondering if he should point that out. Was she making it all up just to get some damned fool to fix her corral?

"He left the gun with me," Rosie said. "I was supposed to shoot anybody coming into the valley. For years I was so scared I would have to do it. I don't know how anybody could have gotten past the house to get in here. I never saw or heard anything. I swear it."

Moving in close suddenly, Del took a firm hold of Rosie's shoulders to keep her steady. He was surprised at how delicate she felt. Her flesh was soft and giving in his hands. He longed to hold her if only to comfort her

"Abner's death wasn't your fault, Rosie. Surely you didn't think that it was," he said.

She shook her head. "Abner was so thin. He had been growing more and more feeble. The doctor told him to give up his work, but Abner wouldn't listen."

"Abner saw a doctor? The doctor knew what Abner was doing?" Del was surprised.

"He thought Abner was prospecting." She actually smiled a little. "Everybody did. Abner had hands like a hard-rock miner. He had everybody fooled. I tried to make him rest, but it was no use. The weaker he got, the harder and longer he worked. He was driven… to do whatever he did here. Find things. Take notes. He died doing what he loved. I try to remember that. It was just hard… getting his body to town."

Her eyes went wide again. Without thinking, Del pulled her close for an tight embrace intended to sooth her soul. He relished the feel of her sagging against him. She smelled like sunshine. He resisted kissing her hair.

"You did a brave thing, Rosie," he said. "I don't know how you got him out of here. That passageway we came through is so narrow."

"I took the posts from the lean-to and made something I had seen Indians use, a drag-litter. I tied him to it and put the poles on my shoulders and dragged him out." She burst into tears.

Del let her sob, anguished to hear her, afraid she would die crying, but then she stopped abruptly. She heaved a ragged sigh, jerked away from him and squared her shoulders. The wind dried her tears. She threw back her head and pinned him with that determined blue stare of hers.

His heart thrilled to see it.

"I was so damned tired after getting him home and into the buckboard I had to wait for the next day to drive him into town. They buried him in the mission cemetery. Someone suggested I move into town, but I couldn't. I can't! I can't leave this place unprotected. What would I do in town, wait for people to ransack Abner's treasure?"

"Who suggested you to move into town?" Del marveled at her transformation. She was incredible, he thought.

"I don't remember now," she said. "I was numb. I didn't cry. I thought I'd just go on living at the house, doing what I have always done. I swore I wouldn't leave. You can see that, can't you? I'm not crazy to stay. Then…" She looked down and away, her mouth tight again. She spoke softly, as if she were ashamed. "But then I had that dream. I was bringing Abner some food, but couldn't find my way. The trail changed. I couldn't seem to see it. The rocks kept sinking and moving and tumbling around me. Then I saw him and when I touched him…" She gave a shudder. The expression on her face showed horror. "I saw my own face. I woke up realizing I was next to die."

All this because of a dream, Del thought. He had married a stranger because she had a bad dream.

"Rosie," he said in his gentlest tone. "Explain why you thought Abner was killed. What did you see, exactly? Just his face? He might've been in pain when he died. Didn't you say he was murdered to get me to marry you?"

Five

Rosie's eyes flew wide. "How can you say that?" she cried, jerking away from him.

"Are you certain there's nothing else valuable about this land?" Del persisted. "I've heard talk they expect to find copper in the territory," he said. "Did anyone besides Wesley Morris approach you after the funeral, wanting to buy the land?"

She just glared at him.

He asked again. "Did anyone offer to buy the land while Abner was alive?"

"I don't remember."

"Then I think Abner told you he was afraid somebody wanted to kill him in order to keep *you* from leaving him. Isn't that all this is?"

With her eyes full of tears, she stared at him, speechless with rage. But then, slowly, she began to look confused. She looked around as if realizing for the first time that she was alone in the isolated canyon with him, an accusing stranger.

Del was bigger and stronger. He watched fear dawn in her eyes.

"I think…" she said softly, struggling to find an explanation amid the jumble of her aching emotions, "I think, because Abner wasn't there to tell me what to do, I… I realized I'd never be able to talk to him again. When I came back after the funeral, the house was so empty. Everything in the house was his, but he was gone. The silence went on all day. All night. I was so alone."

Rosie felt desolate in her aloneness. Standing there with her Mr. Grant, she still felt her aloneness like a yawning space enveloping her, threatening to swallow her.

Mr. Grant nodded, his eyes squinting, his expression grave. "I understand, Rosie," he said gently. "I understand exactly what you mean."

She shook her head. He was trying, but he didn't understand. He couldn't. He was a man. He was strong. He knew how to defend himself. He couldn't know what it felt like to be a little girl and have everyone she knew and loved dead.

He reached toward her, but she backed away, afraid to depend on his strength again. She dared not let him touch her. She didn't know what she would feel if he did.

"My parents died," she whispered, shaking her head, loath to remember that awful time. "I was eight. It was in a mill town, I think. My papa worked in a mill… I remember a dark room. We were always hungry. I don't…. all I remember sometimes is the sound of my papa's voice. Or Mama holding me. They must've been sick. I don't know. There was no help. No food. It got cold. There they were… just laying there, coughing. Days went by. No one came. I didn't know what to do. I was so little. I wanted to hide."

Rosie wasn't sure what to make of Mr. Grant's ragged expression. His brow was so low over his eyes. His eyes looked like glass, glinting and sharp. He held his mouth like is was full of broken glass.

"What happened then?" he asked in a soft tone.

"Someone came. A preacher, I think. He took me to the orphans' home," she said, battling tears all over again. "They taught me to read and do chores. But I never learned to cook." Her sudden shaking laughter sounded loud and false. It was a nervous attempt to dismantle her anguish. "I was ten when I went to work in the mill. My job was to keep the needles threaded. There were hundreds of needles. My hands were small. I could reach in... the shuttles moved fast. Gears going around. The thrashing sound of the heddles. Up and down. Very fast. Very loud."

She shuddered, remembering. She hadn't thought of that in such a long time.

"I had to be careful," she went on. "The looms were like monsters. We were afraid, us girls. The machines ate fingers, smashed hands. If you got hurt you'd never work again. You'd starve. Careful! Careful!" She balled her fists. "I had to get away from that! You can see that, can't you? I wasn't crazy to marry myself to a stranger."

Mr. Grant edged closer. For a moment Rosie couldn't remember who he was. She felt like she was back at the mill, working endlessly.

"Abner was murdered," she cried, defiantly. "I know it!"

But Rosie's belief in that had been shaken. What if... what if Abner had just... died? What if no one was trying to kill her? She would have no further need of a protector, a gunfighter, a husband.

Now she could easily imagine Abner staggering around, dying from a stroke rather than fighting off a murderer. Who would've come into the box canyon anyway? An intruder couldn't carry away a wall of cliff dwellings. There was no treasure to steal that she knew of. Why did Abner fear someone finding the ruins? Did he simply not want to share them?

Rosie covered her face with trembling hands. She felt like a fool.

Then the truth settled upon her turbulent thoughts like a feather. She went soft all over, realizing the simplicity of it. She uncovered her eyes. She met Mr. Grant's penetrating stare. It had been that dream.

"I didn't want to be alone again," she said. "I *never* would have left Abner. Where would I have gone? He was all I had. There he was, dead. I felt so angry… He left *me!* Don't you see? He couldn't have just… died!" she cried. "He had to have been killed!"

Del watched Rosie struggle to get those heartrending words out. She looked so young, so vulnerable. It hurt him to see her pain. He understood how she felt. He was alone like that, too.

But he still had a job to do, he reminded himself suddenly. He had been doing it more than a week now, or trying to. But faced with this helpless side of Rosie, Del realized he cared what happened to her. It was already too late. He couldn't leave her now. Everything had changed.

"I'm sorry," he managed to say. "If Abner was murdered, or even if he just died, I'll stay with you."

He was such a liar, he thought. He hated himself for leading her on.

Del ground his teeth. He hoped his words sounded businesslike. Nothing had really changed, he told himself. He would stay with her, and see her safe. Mentally he stepped away from her. He tried to close whatever felt gaping wide and raw within himself.

He forced himself to say the words. "I want you to consider moving into town, Rosie. I want you to really think about it——" He glanced at her, hating himself. "Don't shake your head. Don't say no. Think about it. Think about having a better life somewhere else. One woman can't protect these ruins. People will find them. It's just a matter of time. I know that's not what you want, but you had to face facts when you were a child. You had to face facts when you found Abner dead. I'll do my best to help you get started somewhere else. You said so yourself, this isn't a real marriage."

He watched the corners of her mouth twitch with scarcely controlled emotion.

"I hired you to help me!" she shouted. "I'll never leave these ruins. There's nothing for me in town. I won't sell. I thought you understood that. I'll die first!"

• • •

They stayed only two hours more at the cliff dwellings. While Mr. Grant climbed up to the base of the main wall, Rosie waited in the shade cast by the eastern ridge. She watched

him, seething, but by noon it was too hot to maintain her
fury. Heat waves made everything look dreamlike. She
felt mesmerized.

She wanted to stay angry, but something between Mr.
Grant and herself had shifted. She couldn't put her finger
on it and felt uneasy. Leaving her resting in the shade of
a cottonwood, he skirted the entire box canyon from the
entrance to the looming walls. She watched how he moved,
taking long strides, looking so healthy, so young. Sometimes
he stopped to study the ground, or pick something up, but
unlike Abner he didn't immediately rush to a journal to
take notes. He dropped his find and moved on, climbing,
exploring, seemingly restless and troubled. He needed to be
paid for the work, she told herself. They had struck a hasty
bargain, and now he was feeling the strain of it. Soon he
would be gone.

Taking a long drink of spring water, she watched him
climb like a big horn sheep, stepping from place to place
with such strength she longed suddenly to be beside him,
exploring. When he ducked into one of the stone dwelling's
doorways she started to worry. She didn't like sitting there
alone in the fading light. The rugged walls of the box
canyon seemed to close in. The whispering wind stirred the
grasses all around her. Unseen forces moved through the air
and rose up from the dry earth. Rosie wondered if the ruins
were haunted.

Like a spooked horse, she jumped to her feet and ran.
Panic gripped her so completely she didn't know anything
but her shoes hitting the dirt. It was farther to the ruins than
it looked. Gasping for breath, she started climbing, startled
to find herself as strong and agile as Mr. Grant looked,

climbing from the canyon floor to the lower doorways. She had never been so close before. She had never yearned to go inside as Abner had. There had been so much Abner had wanted to show her. She had always refused, as if stepping through one of those dark doorways was like being back in the mill, or worse, back in that tenement room.

The rock wall loomed two hundred feet above her, high into the brow of rock overhead. The slope was steep. The wind moaned and pulled at her hair, whipping it around like her uncontrollable thoughts. Her skirts tangled around her ankles. Pulling up her hem, she stepped from place to place as she had seen Mr. Grant do.

Frantic to find him, she ducked into the nearest stone doorway where she had seen Mr. Grant disappear. She came up short, panting. Inside, the small, stone-walled room was hushed and empty. It smelled dry like rock. Like time unending. Cool and strangely peaceful. In deep dark shade. Like dreamless sleep. The smooth dirt floor was covered in a fine layer of rubble and felt slightly slanted beneath her feet. She planted her feet and listened to the absolute absence of everything. Above were thick log beams so pale with age she could not imagine they could support any of the weight above. A mental image of the bluff crushing her made her duck down suddenly and cover her head with her arms. She felt at one with the dirt and rock and rubble already. There was an opening in the ceiling, another doorway nearby.

She was going to be buried in there forever! *Get out! Get out now!*

"Mr. Grant?" she called out. Her voice was muffled by the thick stone walls.

Struggling to breathe, she fought the urge to scream.

Hearing footsteps echo, she fled the stone-walled room, back into the blazing sunshine. She saw Mr. Grant duck out from another doorway some distance away. She ran toward him, slipping on the gravel path, scraping her elbow and her palm as she fought for balance. She had to get close to him. She needed him to take her hand.

Surprised to see her, Mr. Grant halted and reached out. "Are you all right, Rosie?" His eyes were so clear, so crystal blue, like beacons in his tanned face.

She grabbed his hand and felt the leap of current between them. "Just skittish," she said, startled, quick to let go and hold herself back. "Did you find anything?"

He shook his head and stepped away. She wondered if he realized what a handsome man he was. She wished he would take her in his arms and hold her just until she felt more steady.

"We should eat and then start back," he said. "It must be past noon. You're sure no one ever tried to buy the land before Abner died?"

"When we went to town, if Mr. Morris was there, he would say, 'Found any gold yet, old man?' And he'd laugh as he if he thought Abner was stupid. Abner would act like he was a discouraged old prospector, having no luck. He surely looked the part. We would laugh together on the way home in the buckboard. 'Fooled that buzzard,' Abner would say. He wanted folks to believe the land was worthless. If anyone came here, I think Abner would have killed *them*."

She watched Mr. Grant cock his head as he considered that. The sunlight turned his skin golden. His lips worked over his teeth. He gazed up at the sky and the looming bluff and the ruins standing so massive and silent. Then he fixed his eyes on her.

"Did you ever regret marrying Abner?"

She squirmed beneath his gaze, afraid he could see inside her to the softness.

"Not at first. I feared he might change his mind about being married to me and try to send me back… but after a year I realized he didn't see me as a wife. I was his cook, his housekeeper. Then, sometimes, I was sorry. But he was always kind to me," she put in quickly. "He tried talking to me, but I didn't understand."

Mr. Grant extended his hand again. His expression had softened. She was so surprised, she grabbed it. He felt so strong, so solid, not tremulous or bone-thin like Abner. Awareness of him as a man swept through her. Trying to ignore it, she held on tight as she made her way down the rubble-strewn foot of the cliff dwellings to the floor of the rocky box canyon.

As soon as she was steady on her feet again, Mr. Grant let her go. He strode on ahead by himself, putting distance between them. By the time she caught up to him he had the canteen out and had drained nearly half of it.

When she drank from it, the water was most welcome. As they walked back to the cottonwood where she had left their supplies, she pointed out rock formations Abner had told her about. But she wasn't thinking of Abner anymore. She thought about Del Grant, her husband, as he stepped along beside her, listening, nodding, his eyes intent on her as she spoke. His attention wasn't on a rock or a shard or an artifact. His attention was on her.

Longing to ask what was bothering him, she watched him refill the canteen from the shallow pool. Falling silent, she feared more questions would ruin this ease that had settled between them. There seemed to be a delicate balance between them now. She dared not spoil it. She had a feeling they didn't have much time left to be together. Now that he had seen the ruins, she sensed he wanted to be gone.

• • •

That evening as Rosie tried not to burn the beans and made flour tortillas on her cook stove, Del gathered everything that had belonged to Abner and carried it out of the room where he had been sleeping. Outside, he buried the boxes of artifacts and the books in a shallow depression just beyond the spring. He stored the journals under a slab of rock some distance away from that. Why he did it, he couldn't have said. Maybe he was trying to bury Abner's memory.

He stood awhile, listening, sniffing the breeze, studying every hillock, every rocky ravine. He saw nothing out of the ordinary. No one was interested in this place, he told himself. Abner Saladay had been a mistrustful eccentric, and Rosie had been his unwitting prisoner. Del had become entangled in a web of greed on Wesley Morris' part. He longed to forget about Rosie and be away. Headed home, he reminded himself. Well, no. Not home. That was just his story. Just away from all that Rosie made him feel and want.

After stripping everything from the plank bed in Abner's old room, in his own room now, Del punched the sand-filled mattress into a better shape and laid out the clean change of bed linen. Then he took the blankets out to the barn. For the better part of an hour he beat the dust from them with a piece of stout kindling. It felt good to hit something again and again. He kept reminding himself he was not the man of this house. He was just the hired hand.

When Del went back inside, he found the beans and tortillas lying cold on his plate. He hadn't realized he had been outside so long. Rosie had swept the hard-packed dirt floor of his room. That left a faint pall of fine dirt hanging in the air. She had dragged Abner's trunk to the doorway. She looked peculiar now, sitting on her stool, staring transfixed at the low fire in the adobe fireplace. She looked tired, yes. Worried, maybe. Forlorn, definitely. He sat and ate in silence. He should say something, he thought, but he was just a hired husband. *Remember that, Del. Nothing more. Guardian to a crazy widow woman. Just do the job, somehow.* He felt like throwing his plate across the room.

"You should sell Abner's things," he finally said of the trunk and threadbare clothes in it. "In a couple of days we can take everything to town. Trade for things you need. Food. A new outfit, maybe. I have a little money you're welcome to."

She just looked at him, her expression slack.

"I'll be riding out early tomorrow morning, up to the ridge, to scout for game," he continued. He felt starved for fresh meat.

She nodded, seemingly relieved that he was talking, that he wasn't angry. She seemed different now, vulnerable, even a little helpless. He didn't like it. What was wrong with her?

After he said goodnight and went into his room—*his room finally*—he felt better for a time. He sat on the ungiving edge of the bed, thinking about where he was going to cut a window in the adobe wall and frame it.

In his hands, he had the last journal Abner had been writing in before he died. He had tucked it inside his shirt when they started back from the ruins that day. Now Del looked at it, thinking he should have put it out under that rock with the others. He turned the pages carefully. Abner's entries focused on the artifacts he had been unearthing in a particular room of the ruins. All Del could think was that the man had been working at the ruins an awfully long time. To what end?

The ruins had mystery, beauty, and historical value, but even Rosie wasn't dedicated to them. She was dedicated to Abner Saladay. This house was a grave.

No matter how much work he did, this would never be his place. He didn't belong here.

He tossed the journal aside and laid back on the bed. The sand shifted beneath his back. He lay in a depression that fit him now. He knew the shadows of the ceiling. He knew the rush of the wind outside. He knew the smell of the warm earth and the wood smoke and the scent of Rosie's hair when she edged around him to pour coffee in the morning. He knew what he felt about her when night came on. He was a man, wasn't he? He wanted her.

He listened to the sounds she made when she banked the fireplace for the night, her feet on the floor, the rustle of her skirts, and then she slipped behind that curtained doorway. He heard ropes creak as she lay down in her bed. Did the bed have a mattress hard-packed with sand or a feather-filled tick that cradled her body? Did she lie awake listening to him?

• • •

Does he think about me when he's lying in bed at night? Rosie wondered, lying stiffly in her bed.

She kicked off her thin cover and lay in the suffocating room with its rug-covered walls and hard-packed floor. She wished for a window and fresh air. Sometimes the heat was so unbearable in her room she couldn't think. She was tired now, sore after riding to the ruins and climbing around. She turned over, wishing for a new pillow. Suddenly she longed for so many things, a new dress, a petticoat with deep flounces, a pair of shoes that fit. She felt confused. She felt terribly unhappy.

"Mr. Grant?" she called into the darkness, her heart hammering.

"What is it?"

"Do you really think Abner made up his fear of being discovered and robbed just to hold me here?"

"I'm sorry I said that, Rosie."

"I'm sorry your supper was cold."

She waited.

He didn't answer for a long time. "I wish I could help you more with that," he finally said.

"I don't like my cooking either," she said and smiled.

She liked his gentle honesty. As she struggled to think of something more to say from the darkness and safety of her room, she heard Mr. Grant beginning to snore. She covered her face with hands that felt cold. She couldn't allow herself to feel this way. The minute Mr. Grant realized she was having girlish fancies about him, he would ride away. She was sure of it.

In the morning, Rosie's worries of the night before seemed foolish indeed. She got up early and was already weaving on her latest basket when Mr. Grant came out of his room with his hair tousled and his face still dumb with sleep. Her heart rolled over at the sight of him. He was becoming a part of her life. Trying to hide her blossoming feelings, she forced herself not to jump up to heat coffee. She resumed weaving, her fingers clumsy and her mouth dry. What had ever made her think she could make such an arrangement work? She didn't know how to be married to a real man.

Mr. Grant watched her for a moment, his expression thoughtful.

"Where did you learn to do that?" he asked, scratching the back of his neck.

She smiled to think he noticed her work. "From the baskets Abner brought from the ruins. He showed me how they were woven. I found it easy to copy them. Later he changed his mind about having the ancient pieces here. He didn't want anyone coming here and seeing them... and guessing there were ruins nearby. He took them all back."

"They're nice," he said, giving her a slight smile.

Glowing inside, she watched her Mr. Grant go outside.

When she heard him ride away, her heart sank. He hadn't eaten anything! It was just like when Abner left the house without speaking so much as a word. Running to the door, fighting the urge to call out to him, Rosie watched Mr. Grant gallop away. Let him ride off without a word, she thought. She dashed away sudden tears. *Let him hunt all day without me. I can endure it. I can endure anything.*

Except losing him.

Rosie let herself admit it.

She was falling in love with her husband.

She drank her coffee on the stool outside, watching, waiting, staring at the place where she had lost sight of him. She didn't eat anything. She didn't think. She just stared at the spot, willing him back like she used to will Abner back. They would have to go to town soon and face the snickers and sly looks. Mr. Wesley Morris would give her that contemptuous stare she hated so. She would pretend to be strong and threaten to shoot anyone who dared to cross her... what did that matter? She just wanted her Mr. Grant back. Anything might happen now, alone there, at the mercy of the whispering wind.

Dear God, she thought, Abner was dead and gone, the dear old fool. She sprang to her feet, wishing she could let out a shout of... what? Anguish? Relief? She was so very glad Abner's obsession with the ruins was at an end. She felt so surprised at herself she almost couldn't breathe. She felt alive!

If there was any critter worth eating within five miles of the house, Del thought, he hadn't seen it. Deer, jackrabbit, squirrel, nothing. He never fired a shot all day. He felt bitterly hungry by the time he returned to the house late in the afternoon. All day he had tried to stay away from Rosie and the sound of her voice, the puzzling look in her eye. To get away from her as quickly as possible, he had gone off without anything to eat. He was acting like a damned fool. *Kiss her and get it over with. What was the worst that could happen?* She had put the gun away, hadn't she?

As he rode up, Rosie was quick to appear in the doorway. He half expected her to have that old gun in hand and greet him with a suspicious scowl, but her expression showed such relief at the sight of him. He felt surprised and a little embarrassed. It warmed his heart to be greeted by so radiant a face. She looked utterly beautiful, smiling like that, but it put him immediately on guard. What was this crazy new emotion of hers, he wondered.

"No luck," he called casually, riding past her into the barn where the shade was welcome.

"I never found much around here when hunting, either," she said, following him.

Del felt her watching his every move as he pulled the saddle from Banjo. *Had something happened during the day?* he wondered. He looked at her and made a quizzical smile. If he didn't know better, he would think—

A twinge of apprehension rushed through Del's stomach.

All right, he cautioned himself. *Don't go getting crazy ideas like she's falling in love with you.* She had been a widow scarcely three weeks. She was just lonely. She was glad he hadn't abandoned her. Or died. *Keep feeling sorry for her.* That had worked so far, he told himself.

"After my first year here I got bold and wandered around a little," she said. "I used to fancy finding more handprints, or something that would please Abner."

He mucked the barn and fed and watered the horses. He washed in the cold spring, cursing that slow dribble of refreshment. She kept following him.

"You found nothing?"

She shook her head, sighing. "One time I found some other stone floors," she said. "Abner said there must've been some kind of settlement here in the valley."

"But the ruins were more to his liking?"

"Whatever was built here wasn't as old, he told me." She walked alongside him back to the house, pointing toward the south. "I could show you, if you're interested."

"I'm more interested in watching you weave one of those baskets," he said, itching to snatch at the pins holding back her hair. He wanted to see it tumble free. He wanted to feel those gleaming strands slip through his fingers.

"All right," she said, pinking with pleasure. "Now? I didn't get much done today."

Nodding, he followed her inside.

While he sat on the stool, she settled herself on the floor in a pool of sunlight falling through the nine-light window. He listened to the sound of her voice as she described how she held the grasses and slowly wove them back and forth to achieve her pattern. She told him about gathering minerals to make her own dye, and laughed as she wiggled fingers stained by those dyes. But he didn't retain anything she said. He was memorizing the delicacy of her hands, the way her wrists looked so slender as she wove the grass, how her face grew serene with concentration, how the pattern emerged and made her smile as she held it up for him to see. He wondered when was the last time he had paid close attention to a woman like this.

"Have you always liked working with your hands?" he asked.

"I worked with Mama. She took in sewing. I was too little to sew, but I remember picking stitches. She could make something new from something old."

"You made the woven rug by my bed?"

"I did! That was my biggest project." Then she laughed softly. "I thought it would help Abner keep his socks clean. He never took off his boots. I made the curtains. My skirt." She fell silent a while and then asked, "Hungry?"

"Yes. I was wondering if you'd like a window. You said you helped Abner build the additions. That must've been difficult for you."

Climbing to her feet, she shrugged. "I enjoyed working with him. He really had no idea how to do it. I'd love a window."

"Maybe you can show me where you think it would be safe to poke a hole."

Quickly she served their meal. They were down to porridge with molasses. He had thought she traded for supplies the day they were married, but apparently those few baskets she had traded hadn't brought much. He wondered if the storekeeper was cheating her. One basket represented hours of work.

"Sorry," she said when they were done eating. "I know you're still hungry. We'll have to go to town soon, I guess."

"I should have helped you buy more supplies. I guess we were in some kind of crazy hurry that day we got married."

"I guess we were," she said, blushing a little.

They sat in silence a while longer. When she finally asked if he had seen anything of interest while out riding, his only remark was that he couldn't see the cliff dwellings no matter how close he got to the rim of the bluff.

"It was eerie," he said, "knowing the cliff dwellings were right there under my feet almost. I wonder if anyone else ever stumbled upon them. It's beautiful country, but a person can't really make a living out here with so little water for fishing, and no game. I kept wondering why those ancient people settled here, what their lives were like. It's hard to imagine a time so far back."

And then like clockwork, the conversation came around to Abner again. Always Abner. How had he found the canyon? How might someone else have found Abner there... if he had been found? How many years back did the cliff dwellings date? A hundred years? A thousand?

They chewed that subject until they were both bone weary of it.

Still Rosie lingered at the table, seemingly unwilling to let their conversation end. She watched the fire burning low in the fireplace, glanced at him, and then looked quickly back to the fire. Del wondered if she wanted something.

"Did you always live at the orphans' home, even after you went to work in the mill?" he asked.

She got up to clear the table. "Until I was sixteen. Then I lived in a boarding house with other girls who worked at the mill. What about you? Did you always live on the farm?"

Del got up to stoke the fire. "I went away to college. And I was in the war, on the Confederate side." He tried to make light of that. "Lucky to be alive, I think."

She washed their plates with such care Del had to wonder if she was dawdling. She seemed so at ease now he couldn't help but wonder what the harm would be if

CACTUS ROSE

they—if they—*No. No!* He shut off that line of thinking with all the self-discipline that was in him. They couldn't indulge in any sort of intimate contact. No conjugal rights, he reminded himself. She deserved his compliance.

But abruptly, he leaned back on his stool. He was tired of pussyfooting around Rosie all the day long. He was tingling with complete awareness of her and couldn't deny it. It was stifling in there. He had the fire built too high. She looked flushed and beautiful and so desirable he wasn't certain he dared stay a moment longer.

"Were you all right here all day?" he asked, trying to remain casual. *Don't let on how you feel,* he warned himself.

She nodded. "I wished you would've told me where you were going so I wouldn't worry. Or, better still, I would've liked to go with you." She had trouble meeting his eyes.

Something had definitely changed with her, he thought. She didn't seem afraid of him any longer. He grew bold. "I've been thinking..." He felt as awkward as a boy at a cotillion. "After all, we are married..."

Her blue eyes flew wide.

He saw that she understood what he meant and blinked in astonishment. It might have been funny, he supposed, but she looked horrified. He had upset the balance again, dammit.

But how much longer could they go on like this? She wasn't his employer any longer. He was no longer her employee. He was a man. She was a woman. And he wanted her.

But he had misread her just now, he thought, disgusted with himself for making assumptions.

She had become comfortable with him, that was all. She

was glad he was back, safe. She hadn't fallen in love with him.

Feeling like a cad, Del got up from his stool and went outside. The door banged shut behind him. He was sweating. The way she looked, sitting in there, gawking at him, she might send him on his way that very night. That would be all right by him, he thought, kicking the stool half way across the yard. He should get on his horse and go while there was still some light. Before she pulled her gun.

He was hungry enough to leave, that was for certain.

And he was damned hungry enough to stay!

Six

Rosie's hands shook as she followed Mr. Grant outside.

He hadn't really said what she thought he said, had he, she wondered. About being married… as if to suggest they might indulge in something intimate together. He couldn't have meant that, could he? She surely had misheard him. She had been so clear in the beginning. No conjugal rights.

She found Mr. Grant carrying the stool back to the house. He sank down on it, leaned his elbows on his knees and frowned into the darkness. With the only light falling through the open doorway, Rosie could scarcely see his face. All she could make out was the outline of his cheek and his tousled curls. She felt as if she had never stood so close to another human being in her life.

She couldn't speak.

Slowly he turned to look up at her. There was such a puzzling glint in his eyes.

Her intended words were forgotten.

He twisted his body toward her. His hand lifted and

with a smooth motion; he grasped her arm and drew her down to his lap. She felt his arms wrap around her. It all happened so quickly, so easily, she didn't know what to do. She felt herself settle rather stiffly and awkwardly onto his thighs. His hand felt warm as it cupped her cheek and pulled her expertly toward his lips.

Oh, he was trying to kiss her! She didn't remember to resist. It was as if her body and its desire for him had overtaken her.

When his lips touched hers, she was startled by their softness, their warmth. She was astonished by the longing and surprise that blossomed inside herself. For several seconds she knew nothing but being enveloped in his warm embrace, of having his mouth on hers. There were no thoughts, no words, no intentions or expectations. It was just a moment outside time when something happened to her that had never happened before.

When he pulled away, all she could see was the light from the house shining on his forehead and the slope of his nose. His hands were on her still, holding her gently. She could easily get away but she had gone limp in his arms. She wanted to kiss him again!

When Del pulled away from Rosie's lips, all he could see was the shine in her eyes and smell her hair, tumbling free around her shoulders. His head was spinning. Rosie had come out the doorway at just the moment he had felt the most confused about her. Angry with her. Hungry for her. He had been thinking she must know they were at risk of making their arrangement something entirely new. Something like this. He was thinking—

And now here she was in his arms. He wasn't even certain how she got there.

He could feel her trembling as she sat on his lap. She felt so good in his arms. He felt exhilarated. He wanted to kiss her again!

"That was my f-first kiss," she whispered ever so softly.

Had he heard her right? *Oh, no,* Del thought, torn now by more confusion. That couldn't be. Abner had never kissed her? He just…

And then the truth of what Rosie had just said washed over him. He felt himself go weak with realization. Abner had never consummated their marriage. The old fool.

"You mean, you were never kissed like that—" he said softly, wanting to be sure he heard her right.

Rosie shook her head, solemnly, like she was admitting a terrible truth.

"Not kissed? Ever? Not even before you came here?" he asked. "There must've been others. There had to be."

What made him say such a thing, he wondered. Had he assumed, somewhere in his tangle of thoughts, that there had been a failed romance back east and that was why Rosie had come so far west and stayed so long with Abner?

In that saloon she had seemed as hard-bitten and determined as any woman he had ever met.

Rosie shook her head again. She looked so earnest. And something more. She glanced up at him, looking as hungry as he felt.

The longer he stared at her, the more he could feel her getting poised for flight. She was afraid of her own feelings, he thought. He felt as if he were holding onto a wild untamed creature who had crept up to him in trust ever so briefly and might at any moment jump up and flee.

And never come back.

"There were a few men at the factory who tried to kiss me," she said, "and more, but I managed to keep away from them."

Her words swirled around in the darkness that was overtaking Del's sense of reason. Her gaze became intent upon him. The longer she looked into his eyes, the more urgent Del's situation became. He dared say nothing more.

If he was to maintain their non-intimate arrangement, he was certain he must never kiss her again. He must put her from him, get up, and leave!

She began to grow stiff in his arms. She was trying to get up now. He relaxed his hold and felt her climb awkwardly to her feet. He could see her face. He could see the question in her eyes, the soft vulnerability of her mouth. He wanted to kiss her again. And so, so much more.

It was just the two of them in the darkness now, he thought. Anything might happen.

After a time she moved back into the house. She started to close the door, but he was behind her in an instant, catching hold of her again and turning her into his arms. She felt soft and giving against him. He could smell her hair. He wanted to bury his face in her neck.

He hadn't realized how much taller he was than Rosie. He felt suddenly virile and protective at once. She had never seemed this close before. She felt warm against his hands. He could feel her breathing. At such an intimate sound he forgot everything as he tipped up her face and found her mouth again.

He was lost in her. He kissed her even though he knew he should not kiss her, and she let him, trembling and willing. He kissed her harder, deeper, urgently. He felt her give in and melt against him, eager and responsive. Desire had never swept over him so powerfully before this. This was something new and different for Del. Desire made him throw aside his thoughts and defy his own intentions. They were married, after all, he told himself. What was the harm in kissing his wife?

He wanted her now. He wanted Rosie with all the intensity he had ever known. He almost shuddered with the sense of power coursing through his veins. She started, struggling suddenly, violently, making frightened little sounds that sent ice through his pulsing veins. He opened his eyes. Rosie's face looked contorted with fear. Oh, not fear. Don't fear me, Del thought, relaxing his hold.

"Rosie," he whispered softly. "Don't fight me. It's all right."

But it wasn't all right. There was something... something...

She pushed him away.

"No!" she whispered. "I told you, no conjugal—"

"Where did you ever hear such a fancy word as that?" he teased softly, craning his neck to find her mouth again. His lips found her neck, her throat. Her skin was like silk. He wanted to play and romp with her. He wanted to make her laugh with pleasure. *Smile!* he wanted to say. *Want me!*

"Abner—" She was gasping in panic. "He... he was always saying no conjugal union. No... Too... He said he was too... old. He didn't want me to catch his lung fever."

Del wondered if she had begged Abner for affection and been refused. Regaining a scrap of self-control, he had to let her go. This was too soon. Too much for an inexperienced woman. He did not intend to terrify her.

Del enveloped her once again in his arms ever so gently to calm her. He wanted to bring a smile to her lips, but when he looked into her face again he still saw only dread. His heart sank. This was going so badly, he thought. He stepped away, cold suddenly. Hurt and trying valiantly to hide it.

"Rosie," he spoke softly, tenderly. "I'm not going to… It's all right. Relax—"

He caught himself. An endearment had been on the tip of his tongue, but he caught it in time. *Dear.*

"I just can't," she whispered so softly he almost couldn't hear her. "Del, please. I don't know how."

At first all Del knew was that Rosie had called him by name. It felt like a prize. His chest swelled with pleasure. He gathered her up as tenderly as he knew how, and kissed the top of her head where her soft hair gleamed in the lamplight. *Dear*, he thought. *Dear.* He stroked her back, soothing her. Rosie had come west to a husband who only wanted her to work. She had never been Abner's real wife. And back east she had avoided men. Rosie… was still a virgin.

Feeling as if Rosie were made of glass, Del released her and stood back from her a little, not angrily this time, no longer hurt, but with what he hoped was a reassuring smile. He saw her with new understanding. In some ways she was still a girl. He studied her sweet face. Her expression was a mixture of shame and proud defiance.

"He never made love to you?" Del asked softly.

She scarcely moved her head. "No."

114

Now he dared not touch her. If they made love, their arrangement would become a true marriage and it would mean everything in the world to her. It would mean everything in the world to him.

Rosie looked away. Then she looked back at him nakedly, very much the way she had that first day in the saloon. He dared not take advantage. Despite all she had said, all that she had insisted upon, he could see that she was disappointed. She wanted him now, and he could not comply.

Well, what was done was done, he thought. He would not apologize for being a gentleman. He wasn't sorry he had kissed her. He was just sorry it had changed everything. He felt his own expression harden, his body tensed anew. It might be easier if she slapped him, he thought, but she didn't. At least she didn't say she was sorry she had kissed him back. That was something, he thought.

Del didn't know what to do.

"Good night then," she said quietly as she turned her head aside and moved quickly behind the curtain to her bedroom.

She hadn't called him any sort of name that time. Not Mr. Grant. Or Del. Nothing. She just disappeared into the darkness, leaving him standing there with his thoughts. He had succeeded in making her trust him, but he was playing an unpleasant game he longed to put to an end. Why didn't he?

• • •

The next morning Rosie scrubbed Del's shirt in the washtub as if trying to scrub away her own thoughts. She pictured him living there at the ranch house with her, the two of them truly man and wife. She imagined the two of them in bed together, making love, making babies, living as she had dreamed of living so hopelessly with Abner for so many years.

But somehow she had scared away her Mr. Grant— Del—the night before. She wanted him to stay with her for good but they couldn't raise a family on her basket weaving. She couldn't live off the earnings of a gunfighter. She couldn't imagine raising a family in her dirty, suffocating ranch house. Or abandoning the damnable ruins.

When Del came outside and saw her hanging his shirt on the line behind the barn where it dried in the wind in less than a few minutes, she blurted out before she could think, "What were you doing in that saloon that day?"

Why had he been there? She had wondered that so many times. What she meant was, what had he been doing the day *before* she met him, before he gambled away all his money and had so much to drink that he just slept in the saloon's corner? How could she love a man like that?

At her unexpected question, Del regarded her with a peculiar light in his eyes. He seemed to be studying her. She felt exposed and uncomfortable beneath his gaze. His poker face settled over his handsome features. Oh, how she hated that blank expression!

He headed for the spring. "And good morning to you, too, Mrs. Grant."

Whenever she asked something he didn't want to answer, he walked away from her. This time she refused to follow. When he came into sight again, his hair was dripping. He looked like he was engrossed in important thoughts that did not include her just like Abner used to look. She wanted to grab him and shake him.

What did it matter if she angered him, she wondered. She might as well persist. He owed her. He owed her more than he had offered up so far about himself.

"Who is back east that you want to go home to see... but are afraid to see?" she asked, thinking herself perceptive and bold.

Ah, there, she thought with a small sense of triumph. She had surprised him. He hated to talk about himself. Her curiosity began to rage.

"You've got it wrong, Rosie," he said with maddening calm. "There's no one back home waiting for me... or not waiting for me. I'm just not needed there. I didn't fit there any more than I fit... here."

He seemed ready to march into the barn to feed the horses, but stood still a moment as if considering something more to say. He didn't speak, but something hung in the air between them. Rosie felt transfixed, waiting. This time he wasn't walking away.

"It wasn't exactly a farm I grew up on, Rosie. It was more like a plantation. I have an older brother," he said. "He was supposed to inherit. I... as second son... meant nothing to my father. My brother was the important one, taller, smarter, more dutiful. I was always making mistakes, getting into trouble, disappointing everyone. My brother did everything my father asked of him. And he did everything very well. I looked up to my brother. I admired him. I wanted to be like him." His voice broke. "I wanted to be loved as he was loved."

Rosie's heart rolled over. She had not expected Del to say so much. She hadn't known men longed for love as she had done all her life.

"All my life I've been doing things I didn't want to do. My brother did everything asked of him. I would do the opposite. He excelled with the tutors. I pretended to be dumb ignorant." He grinned in a strangely bitter way. "It made my father furious. The only thing I ever did right was protect my mother from him."

"Protect her?"

"He knew how to hurt her. With words, mostly, but there were other times. Then she died. It was sudden. She didn't suffer. I missed her, but I was glad she was gone, glad he couldn't hurt her feelings anymore. Can you understand that, Rosie? Glad she wasn't suffering his silences, his insults, his... lack of humanity."

Rosie hurried after Del as he stalked across the sunlit yard and stopped half way back to the house. She wanted to point out that sometimes he tortured her with silence.

"You're right, Rosie. I say I'm going home, but I don't go. I can't go back. The house is gone. The land, too, probably. I earn enough money to go back and find out. Then I gamble it away so I don't have to actually go. There's nothing left there. My home is gone. If I ever had a home."

"I'm sorry," Rosie whispered.

And yet, as sorry as she felt, the question she most wanted to ask came out as if the words had life of their own. "Have you told me any other lies, Del?"

The dark look that Del cast back at her made her blood run cold. There was a long and unsettling pause.

"Lies? I don't consider calling a plantation a farm a lie. No, Rosie," he said as if his words were a challenge. "I have not told you any lies whatsoever." But the expression on

Del's face said so much more.

Rosie shivered in the heat. She wasn't sure of him after all. That flat reply sounded an awful lot like a lie in itself. Was he really the good man she thought he was?

"Do you really want me to stay, Rosie?"

Del's eyes grew intense. He actually looked a little wild and afraid. Afraid to stay, or afraid to go, she wondered.

"Please stay," she whispered, deciding to take a chance on him.

Please reach out to me again, she thought, waiting, breath held, heart filling with hope.

But he only turned away as if he were being held a prisoner.

• • •

Rosie couldn't stand it another hour.

She had to do something! They had avoided each other all day. She had spent the afternoon finishing another basket but making a mess of it. Then it was time to scrape together the last of their beans and mush and thin soup. They would have to go to town in the morning.

The sad thing was, she was going to let him go, she told herself. There was no use holding a man who didn't want to stay. All that was left was for her to decide if she should sell out or stay at the ranch by herself. If she stayed there alone she would die. She was sure of it. It was the first time she had considered the possibility of abandoning Abner's ruins. She felt sick at the very thought.

"Do you think we could try to make that window you were talking about?" she said, rousing Del from his seat by the door.

Sighing, he climbed to his feet and stretched. "Sure."

She described how she and Abner had laid out the foundation stones for the addition and built up the walls.

"So it's all just rocks and dirt and some lumber thrown in for luck?" he asked, following her around to squint and scowl at the crumbling walls. Hummingbirds whizzed around, and a hawk circled in the sky.

"I think if we work carefully, pulling out a little at a time, we could hold up this part…" She fetched a wide piece of wood lying behind the house. "I saved this piece, thinking it would lay across like this." She reached up to show him what she meant.

Together they worked, her holding the wood, him plucking out stones one at a time until quickly, they both got the wood in place before the weight of the roof shifted.

"Better go inside to see how things are holding up in there," he said as the opening grew larger. "Yell, if—Maybe I should go inside instead. I'll be the one buried if the roof caves in."

She nodded. "Good idea. I can dig you out." It was the first time she had teased him, she thought.

Del went inside quickly and gingerly stepped into Rosie's bedchamber. It was roughly the same low small space as his room, except she had a real rope-slung bed frame and a mattress. It looked wide enough for two, he thought, glancing at an open trunk where her clothes lay folded, and a table with a basket holding her hairbrush. Removing one of the rugs covering the wall, he was greeted by a small hole admitting a bright shaft of sunlight into the room. Fresh air flooded in, and there, on the other side, was Rosie's eager face and her slender fingers deftly plucking stones from the wall. Glancing up, wondering if the roof might actually cave in, and planning his escape if it did, Del made sure the wood supporting the top of the window seemed secure. In a few minutes, they had a rough window about a foot square, not unlike the windows he had seen at the ruins.

"I think we've done it," he said, grinning.

Quickly he left her room before he could imagine all he wished might happen there. Outside, he watched her study the wall of her addition. She was a clever woman, he thought, pleased with their effort. When she suddenly threw her shoulder against the wall, testing the strength of it, he steadied her.

"Whoa! You'd better let me do that."

He was relieved to find the wall still solid, and laughed. Sweat stood on her forehead, and her cheeks were pink with a touch of fresh sunburn.

"I'd like very much to kiss you if you won't take it wrong," he said. "I think you know how much I've come to like you."

"I like you too," she said, with a shy smile. On tiptoe, she planted a kiss on his cheek. "Thank you for this!"

He caught hold of her hand. He wanted so much more, but he decided to let her do the approaching next time.

It was late when the fire had burned so low there was nothing left but a red glow deep in the crevices of the hard old kindling in the fireplace. More kindling had been piled high in the corner. Del had righted most of the things that were crooked in the house—the table, the dry sink, her shelves.

Rosie supposed Del was sleeping. It had been a tiring day but she felt surprisingly good.

She blew out the lantern and walked into her room with the weight of her life hanging over her head. Life had been so empty for so long, she thought, so hard, so pointless. Why was she still there, clutching Abner's dream to her breast as if it had been her own dream?

It seemed especially still in her room that night, just as it always was. She smoothed the blankets on her rope-slung bed and thought of all the years of nights she had slept there alone, accepting her lot in life. That was how she had survived working in the mill. All those years, threading the needles, minding the looms, teaching other little girls to do what she had done for so long. That was how she had survived here in the valley.

Now she could look out her little window and breathe in fresh air. She let down her hair and ruffled it. She started to unbutton her shirt.

Del cleared his throat. He stood in her doorway, her curtain held aside with one hand, his face completely in shadow. He made a tall, tantalizing silhouette.

Rosie's heart leapt into her throat. She wanted to move toward him, but she was afraid. Why was she so afraid to reach for what she wanted, she asked herself. Was that how it was done between a man and a woman? Who made the first move?

He stepped into the room and let the curtain fall back into place. The room became dark except for a warm rosy glow peeping in from beneath the curtain. Fresh air drifted in through the window.

When his fingertips touched her arms, she felt a jolt inside that blossomed all through her body like a melting sunrise. She curled into his body, relishing the feel of his hands closing in around her back and pulling her close. Oh, to be enveloped like that. It was the most delicious sensation she could think of.

She heard his breathing coming fast against her ear. And then his mouth was on hers like the night before. Slightly wet, and wonderfully warm. Only this time she knew she would not be pulling away from him no matter how frightened she might become. And he would not be letting her go.

Somehow she found herself lying on her bed with him, sinking into the mattress as if it were a cloud and not layers of dried grass. Del felt solid and strong lying beside her. She found the curve of his face where the stubble made his skin feel rough and manly, and then his strong neck was beneath her fingertips, and the surprising softness of his earlobe, the unexpected silkiness of his hair.

He found the buttons of her shirt and moved his hands over her tentatively, pausing to let her grow used to his touch. By then her thoughts were a blur. She thought she would be afraid and brace herself for things unfamiliar and frightening, but none of this frightened her. She wanted him to touch her. She welcomed every caress as if she had dreamed it a thousand times. When Del came to her, she was more than ready, and although her body did find it unfamiliar, her heart did not. She received him with all of herself.

There was a tiny fraction of a moment when she understood why Abner had refused her entreaties all those years. She realized he had known it would mean too much to her. He had known he would die, leaving her with enough life left in her to savor a moment like this with someone else.

And for that Rosie thanked Abner in that split second before she forgot him completely and forever and let herself belong now to the husband possessing her completely.

Seven

Del opened his eyes with a start. He hadn't dreamed it. There she was, lying beside him with her hair tumbling around her sleeping face. Rosie!

He had made love to her, and it had been more wonderful than he had ever imagined lovemaking could be. He felt as if he had been heading for this moment just as if he had been falling from a cliff for days. He couldn't have stopped this from happening, he thought, and yet it was a mistake nonetheless. Now he was falling from a new and more terrible cliff. He must explain himself immediately, but he didn't move. He scarcely blinked. He just stared at her. Her eyes closed in sleep, that kissable mouth. This moment was too astonishing to disturb. He was just going to lie there and look at her all the rest of the day. And make love to her if she would have him again.

Even looking at her spelled danger for him, he thought. He wanted now to touch her cheek, her slim white shoulder, and all the rest of her and relish her response. The fullness of his desire became immediately apparent. When she opened her eyes, blue like morning, he could see the instantaneous sparkle of surprise in them as she blinked, too, startled to find him awake and gazing at her.

"Good morning," she said in a light, happy voice he did not recognize.

A smile spread across her face that warmed Del's heart. She was all right, he thought. He hadn't hurt her. He hadn't ruined this blossoming thing between them. He felt happy, indescribably happy.

Disturb this precious moment with anything but intimate looks and tentative smiles? he thought. He would not do it. There would be time enough for truth later. He pushed reality away. This felt more real than truth. This was a new truth dawning, blotting out all that had gone before. He loved her, and that was all that mattered.

Rosie looked into Del's soulful eyes and wondered if she had died the night before and been reborn. To wake with him in her bed, warm and relaxed beside him, was more than she could have ever hoped for. At last she felt wanted and safe.

He studied her face. She didn't mind it now. She watched his eyes move, those wonderful crystal blue eyes. She watched them caressing the look of her tousled hair, tracing her cheek... she felt something blossom inside herself.

He kissed her.

His lips felt soft and gentle on her mouth. The magic was still alive between them.

A new day had dawned. All she knew was the warmth of Del's urgent mouth on hers, and the touch of his hands as they found her and pulled her close again. Before long she had no consciousness at all except for the union of spirits she felt when they became one. This was how she wanted to be forever.

• • •

She felt married, really married now, Rosie thought as she loaded her newly woven baskets into the back of the buckboard. She was surprised she had managed to make so many in the weeks since Del had been with her. The hours of weaving had slipped by unnoticed, so completely absorbed she had been in her thoughts about him.

Del had already loaded Abner's trunk into the buckboard. She had bundled Abner's clothes separately. She had Abner's gold watch to sell, too, a good one he had rarely looked at. What had he needed a timepiece for at his cliff dwellings? He should have sold it years before when they needed cash for supplies. She certainly didn't need a watch now. She needed food to prepare for herself and her new husband… her real husband.

Exulting, Rosie wanted to twirl around like a girl. She begrudged the hours needed to drive into town and back. All she really wanted to do was to lie beside Del again and look into those wonderful crystal blue eyes of his. To look into his eyes thrilled her almost beyond endurance.

Unable to wash the black dye from her only bonnet, she had thrown it away and woven herself a new one that she hoped would protect her face from the hot sun long enough to get to town and back. A strong wind might blow it apart, so delicate was the weave. But it felt good to wear something new and becoming.

Back inside, she put on the clothes she came west in because they weren't tattered. The shirtwaist and skirt fit loosely now. The jacket was overly warm and probably out of style, but that didn't matter. When she knotted her hair that morning in front of the looking glass, she worried she might look old. But Del seemed not to notice how the wind and years had worn away the girlish curve of her cheek.

"Are you ready?" she called, presenting herself in the main room where everything looked so tidy.

"Almost," Del said, coming inside to change into fresh clothes now that his chores were done.

Del buttoned his spare shirt and stuffed the tail of it into his loose denim trousers. He was thinner. They had nearly starved in the last few days, but he felt as nourished inside as if he had been feasting every night.

He lifted his freshly shaved face and peered at himself in Rosie's looking glass. He seemed different. He leaned in closer. A faint smile tugging at the corner of his mouth. Yep, that was it. He felt sheepishly happy.

"Yes, I'm ready," he said.

When he strapped on his gun belt it felt out of place. In that moment he didn't feel like a gunfighter any longer. Truth be told, he had never been a gunfighter. He had been more of a guard, he told himself. A shotgun messenger on a stagecoach once. A deputy, briefly. That had ended badly.

He shook off the memory. That life was over. He felt changed. No more going off half-cocked when things went wrong. No more reckless decisions… although his latest reckless decision—marrying Rosie—had turned out to be the best decision of his life.

The main room of the ugly dirt house still felt too stuffy

and confining for comfort, but as Del came out of his room he knew he looked better. He used to have a darkness to his face, he thought, a hostility to his gaze that he hadn't been particularly proud of. Such an expression had served a purpose in the past. It had once protected his mother. It had sometimes kept his father at bay. Later, after the war, it got him work. It kept men away who might otherwise start expecting him to fit in somewhere, to explain where he was from, or where he was going. None of that seemed to matter anymore. He couldn't remember why he had felt so ashamed all his life, ashamed that he wasn't like his father or brother. He was glad he wasn't like them.

"It'll be a long ride," he said. "We might be awfully tired when we get back."

He fought a smile. He would much rather stay… home. He tested the word, whispering it softly to himself. Home.

He could take a bit of good-natured ribbing from the townsmen about being a hired husband, he was certain. That didn't worry him anymore. But going to town held hazards he wished he could forget about.

Being with Rosie made him happy. What was so wrong with trying to get her to give up this desert valley and try life someplace else? She didn't know anything of the country. There were so many towns, so many states… why not take her back east… just to see if…

Del shook his head. Maybe he would talk to her about it on the way into town.

As they climbed aboard the buckboard a few moments later, Del felt uneasy. There were no clouds in the high blue sky, but he felt as if a storm was brewing.

"Got your list?" he asked with false brightness.

"Right here," she said, patting her handbag.

Rosie looked wonderfully pretty in her new hat and traveling clothes that were too heavy for hot desert life. She looked younger when her face lit up the moment she saw him.

"I wish we didn't have to go."

He grinned. His gaze swept over her. It was nice that she felt the same as he did.

He pulled her into his arms as he had wanted to do so many times in the past few days. Now she came to him easily. He found it really hard to kiss a woman while grinning. He laughed as he pulled away. She made him forget everything.

"That's the first time I've heard you laugh like that," she said, looking flushed.

"You've heard me laugh," he said, forgetting his dread of the trip. Everything would be all right, he told himself.

"You were laughing at me before," she said, but she smiled.

"I don't think I look like a gunfighter anymore, do you? I'm only wearing this gun out of habit now, to protect us on the road."

"What do you feel like?"

"A cactus farmer," he said with a wink.

"Well, I don't feel like a widow anymore. What do you think of that?"

"I think it's good."

"Do you want to drive the buckboard today?"

"Yes, ma'am," he said tipping his hat. "I brought Banjo just in case."

"In case of what?"

"In case I see anything worth eating on the way," he

said. "I can't take out after game in a buckboard."

"I want a beef steak at the hotel," Rosie said, adjusting her new hat and arranging her skirts.

He felt a momentary flash of worry leaving the house unattended. Perhaps they should find a dog to keep watch when they were away. A dog would make the ranch house seem all the more like home. It wasn't home, he told himself. It might feel like home for now, but there had to be something better for the both of them. They couldn't stay here forever.

The ride into town proved more enjoyable than Rosie had expected. Del forgot whatever was troubling him, she noticed. It felt so natural to watch his moods now, to worry about what he might be thinking or feeling. But she just couldn't work up the energy to worry that day. She rode along in the hot sunshine, jostling on the seat, hugging Del's arm. When they started back that night, she thought, the buckboard would be loaded with enough food to last for weeks. They would be in bed together all night and every night after that. They would make wonderful, beautiful love as many times as they were able!

As they came into town late that morning, Rosie saw townsmen stop what they were doing in order to stare and whisper about them. Del drove slowly past. She thought about how much had changed since that crazy day she drove into town, determined to find herself a husband so she wouldn't feel so alone in the world. Or die.

Men stood in front of the assay office as always, strangers in the territory, hoping to make a rich gold strike. There stood Mr. Morris in front of the miner's association office, talking to the banker. Her body tensed just to see the man. She ducked her face. There would be no avoiding him now that he knew she and Del were in town. The day they had been married, she had left town without speaking to Mr. Morris about his offer to buy the ranch; he would have something to say about that.

Rosie noticed a man at the livery barn tip his hat toward Del. The man wore a broad smirk that shone through his heavy black beard. She watched Del's face split into a sheepish grin that warmed her heart. Del wasn't ashamed to be married to her. He looked proud. She felt overjoyed.

"I can't seem to stop smiling," Del said, chuckling. "I must look like a new husband."

"This must be what it feels like to be happy," she said quietly.

Del drove the buckboard around the plaza and came to a stop in front of Milt Brummit's general store. If only there was some other place to trade, Rosie thought. Maybe next time they'd go to Tucson. They could make the trip in a couple of days.

As Del helped her down, Rosie heard heavy footsteps on the store's porch. Her heart skipped nervously. She hated to face Mr. Brummit alone. She found him surrounded by a clutter of newly delivered goods, irritable, as usual.

"I have business to attend to, Rosie," Del said without looking at her. "A haircut, for one. Can you manage here?"

"Of course," she said. It was a lie. She didn't want to be alone with Bear Brummit... or anyone else. Having Del to lean on was making her soft. Married or not, she had to keep standing on her own two feet.

"I'll meet you back here in a few minutes. We'll have lunch at the restaurant." Del started away.

Rosie watched Del walk off and thought how absolutely

handsome he looked. She let herself admit it. She loved how he moved, how clear and crystal his eyes were in his tanned face, how his mouth curved into something like a smile but not quite a smile. Don't leave me, she thought. Don't ever leave me.

For just a moment Del glanced back. His eyes were intent on her face. It was as if he couldn't stop staring at her. She felt a rush of love for him so intense suddenly she was taken aback. She felt certain everyone in town could see the glow of it on her face.

"Don't be long," she whispered.

Abner's ghost still stood between them, she thought. The land that brought them together stood between them, too. Maybe she should go away somewhere else with Del, Rosie thought. Maybe she couldn't be completely happy until she had started someplace fresh.

With Del out of sight, Rosie was forced to turn and face Mr. Brummit. The moment their eyes met, she felt the heat of his scowl. He pushed an armload of goods into the startled clerk's hands and swung forward heavily.

Backing away, Rosie steeled herself.

"Morning, Rosie," Mr. Brummit said, scarcely noticing what she had to trade in the buckboard. "You're looking better than you did last I saw you. Buy yourself a new hat, did you?"

"Good morning, Mr. Brummit. Thank you," Rosie said. "I made the hat. If you think others would buy one, I can make more. I have a lot to trade today. Abner's things. And his watch." She felt ashamed suddenly, selling Abner's things so soon after burying him but the funeral seemed like a lifetime ago and she needed supplies. "My larder's empty.

Mr. Grant has quite an appetite."

She sounded false but that didn't matter. The sooner she was done with this chore, the sooner she and Del could go home and be together again. That was all she wanted. To be with Del forever.

Mr. Brummit glanced at her buckboard's load. He nodded without really seeing anything. Abruptly, he stepped down from his store's porch and seized her elbow. "Come inside where we can talk."

She tried to pull away. "Please turn loose of me," she said.

"I'll give you a good price for everything, Rosie. I always have, haven't I?" His tone was reproachful as he guided her inside and released her.

The store was so crowded she couldn't back away from him.

"Freight wagon from Tucson was just here," he explained when she tripped over a heap of bridles.

She handed her shopping list to his clerk. Mr. Brummit sent the lad to unload Rosie's buckboard. Back in his office, he wrote in his ledger while Rosie browsed the store, wondering if she would have trade credit left over for foolishness. She felt like a girl again, wanting sweets and bow ribbons and yards of yellow calico. Everything in the store called to her. She began to forget Mr. Brummit's scowl.

As her purchases mounted on the counter, and the clerk started carrying them out to the buckboard, Rosie remembered the fodder she needed from the livery barn, and the bullets at the gunsmith's. She saw the clerk carry out a whole ham. Her mouth watered. Roast ham. Ham and beans. Ham and eggs. Ham on sourdough bread. Her stomach ached with hunger. It had been a good many years since she had gone so long without a decent meal. Del must be starving, too.

Mr. Brummit took the tally from the clerk, handed over some cash, as change, which looked to be enough for the remainder of her needs in other stores. She asked if the clerk could fetch the fodder and bullets. Mr. Brummit sent the lad out. As the buckboard rolled away toward the livery barn Mr. Brummit moved in close.

Rosie tried to head him off. "I want to thank you, Mr. Brummit," she began. "You've been generous today. I'll bring more baskets... and hats, next time?"

Perhaps she could get away with that simple formality. She smiled good day, hoping to be released with nothing further.

He blocked her way. "Everything going all right out there at your place?"

"Very well, thank you," Rosie said, sounding falsely bright. "Mr. Grant is a great help to me." She hated the way she made it sound as if Del was still her employee, her hired husband, rather than her true husband.

Mr. Brummit's eyes took on a nasty glint.

"Finding much gold, is he?"

"No," she said.

It was hard not to correct folks and say there was no gold mine.

"I don't understand," Mr. Brummit was close enough to touch her now.

Rosie felt herself overheating in her heavy clothes.

"You should've waited for me, Rosie," he whispered. "I was going to wait a decent amount of time. Then I would've courted you proper. I wouldn't have made you go on living out at that dirt-roofed shack, looking for gold that ain't there. Why didn't you wait for me? I ain't so bad, am I? Better'n a stranger, anyway. Sell out, Rosie. You're a damned fool not to. Wesley Morris offered you a fair price. He told me so. You don't have to go hungry with some drifter living off you, making you earn money weaving baskets when he ought to be working. I'd do right by you. I got nice rooms here above the store. I wanted you. You knew I—"

"It's done, Mr. Brummit," Rosie said sharply. "It's done."

Did Mr. Brummit really care all that much for her, Rosie wondered, puzzled by his interest. Over the years she had only seen him once or twice a month. He had never betrayed any personal feelings for her then. Of course, she had been a married woman, but she would have sensed something.

She would never have left Abner for anyone no matter how lonely she might have been. Mr. Brummit was interested in her now because of the land. He had no more feeling for her than he did the goods he bought and sold in his badly organized store. He needed a clerk, a cook, and a housekeeper. She saw no promise of bliss in his bed.

Blushing, Rosie turned away.

"Are we done, Mr. Brummit?" she asked. "Do I owe you anything more?"

He looked like he wanted to say a great deal more, but she pressed past him, out the door.

Out on the porch, Rosie felt a bit sick from the encounter. It seemed hotter than usual. There was no wind. The cottonwoods hung limp. The adobe stores looked bleached and tired standing around the plaza. She didn't see Del anywhere.

Mr. Brummit's clerk was just driving her buckboard back

from the livery barn. It was loaded now with everything on her list. Climbing down, he handed her a box of ammunition from the gunsmith's and disappeared back inside the store.

She knew Bear Brummit was watching from the shadowed doorway.

Across the plaza, Rosie saw Del at last, and her heart leaped with relief. But he was talking to Wesley Morris.

Rosie went still and cold inside with surprise. Did Del know Wesley Morris?

From that distance, it appeared Del was trying to give Mr. Morris something. Mr. Morris refused it. Del threw it to the ground. They were arguing. Shouting. She heard their raised voices but not their words. She resisted the urge to run across the plaza to see what the matter was. If the men were arguing, what could she do about it?

Brummit came out of his store. "What do you really know about that man you married, anyhow?" he asked. "A gunfighter. Liable to do just about anything for money."

"Mind your own business, Mr. Brummit," Rosie snapped, tired of dealing with him and wanting to tear off her jacket and throw it to the ground.

"It ain't natural to hire yourself a man. A *husband*. Folks would understand if you got an annulment," he said. "I would. Send him on his way. It ain't too late."

Rosie found herself shaking. She whirled around. "Delmar Grant is my husband, so folks around here had just better get used to it."

Brummit drew back. "So much for no conjugal rights."

Rosie raised her hand to slap him.

Brummit caught her arm, but his gaze snapped to focus across the plaza. A flicker of puzzlement creased his brow before he looked back at Rosie with a smirk.

Twisting away, Rosie watched as Del turned from Wesley Morris and swung into the nearest adobe saloon. She had never seen him move like that, recklessly, as if he weren't in control of himself. Morris stood there in his big hat, feet planted wide apart like he owned the town. She thought he might be laughing. How she hated the man!

She decided to drive the buckboard around the plaza and wait for Del outside that saloon. She didn't get the chance. Wesley Morris started straight toward her, walking fast, cutting across the plaza to reach her before she could get herself onto the buckboard's seat.

Mr. Morris had probably tried to buy the land from Del and been refused, Rosie told herself. Surely Del said the land was not his to sell even if he was Rosie's wedded husband.

If she ever did sell the land, it wouldn't be to a man trying to buy a gold claim. Morris wouldn't care about ruins. Stupid man. What did he understand of history and the legacy of ancient peoples? He believed in the total destruction of open pit mining.

Those were Abner's words.

Suddenly Rosie couldn't remember why cliff dwellings were so important. What did they matter? She felt responsible for something she didn't understand.

At last she got herself onto the seat. Mr. Morris was out of breath by the time he reached her. She started to drive away but Mr. Morris grabbed Old Belle's harness.

"My dear Mrs. Grant," he panted.

"Good morning, Mr. Morris. Turn loose of my team, if you will. My husband's waiting across the way."

"Is he?"

Mr. Morris had a way of looking at her that made her feel small.

"Just wanted to pay my respects. How's the little bride this fine day?" Mockery flashed in his eyes. "You're some kind of fool, Rosie Saladay Grant. Marrying yourself a stranger. Everyone in town is laughing at you. You're the talk in every saloon in the county. I'm surprised you had the guts to show your face. If I'd done such a fool thing as this, I would've crawled under a rock and died."

Shaking with fury, Rosie tried to drive her team over Mr. Morris' feet. What angered her most was having no idea what to say back to him. How could she best a man like this?

Chuckling, he looked her over slowly as if imaging all sorts of vulgar things. "That no-good drifter doesn't really love you, Rosie. He's just doing a job."

She sensed Mr. Brummit lurking in the doorway. Nervously she looked across the plaza. There was no sign of Del.

"That's right, Mr. Morris," she found herself saying in a menacing tone. "It's the job I married Delmar Grant to do, protect me and my land. And he's doing it."

Mr. Morris was enjoying himself. The toothpick between his teeth irritated her to no end. "Go ahead, Rosie. Ask me what I know about Delmar Grant that you don't know. Ask me. Please, do." His smile fell away. He took the toothpick from between his lips. "Ask me, by God, Rosie! You know I'm going to tell you anyway."

Mr. Brummit had come out onto his porch almost as if he meant to defend her. A startling thought. Were these men going to fight over her? Rosie almost laughed.

"Back inside, Brummit," Mr. Morris barked. "This

is between Miz Grant here and myself. Ain't none of your affair."

Mr. Morris held his tongue until Mr. Brummit melted back into the shadows of his store.

Rosie's heart drummed so hard she felt sick. Mr. Morris seemed awfully sure of himself, she thought, wanting to scream for Del. Wasn't this why she married Del, to be protected from men like Wesley Morris?

"I stood right over there that day you drove into town with Abner's body in the back of this here buckboard," Mr. Morris began. "We helped you bury the ol' fool out at the cemetery. We took up a collection to help pay the undertaker. Brummit, in there, ordered you a real nice headstone all the way from Tucson. It's not even here yet. And here you are, married again. You looked like a lost calf, Rosie. I felt real sorry for you. I said to myself—"

"Do you have something new to say, Mr. Morris?" Rosie snapped. Anybody could hear the quavering in her voice.

"Why, yes, I do, Mrs. Grant. There were a good many men in town the week after that, thinking about you all alone out at your place, grieving, toiling away in the hot sun by yourself. Everybody was worried, but I was the one with a plan. You came into town hell-bent on hiring yourself a husband, I made you another real nice offer for your place. So you wouldn't have to shame yourself by hiring a man to marry you." He stood there looking at her, shaking his head as if he pitied her. Then he stopped smiling. He looked stone cold dead in his eyes. "You let me down, Rosie."

She waited, sick with dread. "I did no such thing."

"You let me down, but I wasn't worried," he went on. "I had me a plan, you see. There was this stranger I met the night before. A man who sometimes takes a few drinks too many and loses his money to men like me in poker games. When he was finally broke, I talked over my plan with him. I offered him wages, and he accepted half in advance. In advance, Rosie. We shook hands on it, him and me. I gave him free rein. Do the agreed job any way he saw fit, and then I would pay him the remainder."

Mr. Morris smiled ever so pleasantly up at Rosie and waited. He seemed to be waiting for her to put together the meaning of his story. "You surprise me, Rosie! I thought you were smarter than this. Listen, woman. I mean to have Abner's gold mine," he said in a loud, firm voice. "I don't take no for an answer, not from any man, and not from some uppity widow woman too stupid to know when a generous man like myself is trying to help."

Rosie struggled to understand. Mr. Morris paid... a man who drank and gambled away his...

"I do believe you are a mule-dumb female after all," Wesley Morris exclaimed with exasperation. "I mean to have your land, Rosie. I mean to pay you a fair price for it. All I needed was somebody to convince you to sell. One way or another. By hook or by crook, as they say. I have no personal designs upon *you* myself, unlike some fools I could name. Are you listening now? I paid Delmar Grant one hundred real American dollars to figure out some way to get you off that land. I never expected him to *marry* you to do it, but I admit that's original. Clever man. Get paid by me. Get paid by you. Who can beat that?"

In a thunderous crash of comprehension, Rosie's heart broke clean in half.

Eight

Rosie held herself very still on the buckboard seat. Her mind raced back to that morning she woke from her terrible dream. She had seen herself dead. The smell of her dead husband had been all around her, filling the ranch house like sinister whispers. It had clung to her and made her think there was someone outside, waiting. Someone had killed Abner. She had been certain she would be next.

She had driven into town like one possessed. She needed a husband and by nightfall she had one. A gambler, gunfighter—whatever Del had first looked like to her—and she had immediately liked the cut of him.

She hadn't known it then, but she understood it now. She had liked Del's looks. She hadn't been able to admit to herself that she wanted a new husband, one she liked. She told herself then she didn't care who Del was, or where he was from. All she had wanted was that he marry her so it would be proper to have him at the ranch protecting Abner's land.

Rosie's heart began to ache. That was why Del married her. To make her sell Abner's land to Wesley Morris.

Shaking with rage, Rosie looked down from her buckboard seat at Mr. Morris still holding her team and watching her with contempt. She hated the little crinkles at the corners of his eyes. She didn't feel afraid of him any longer. He was so far beneath Abner, she couldn't be troubled by him any longer.

She heard Mr. Brummit come out of his store again. He stepped down to the ground and came around the team to offer his hand to her. She just looked at it, wanting to kick it away. What possible help could he offer her now?

"Come inside out of the heat, Rosie," Mr. Brummit said almost gently. "Let me help you."

Rosie stared at Mr. Brummit as if he were a stranger. She glared at Wesley Morris and felt her teeth ache because she was clenching them together so hard. Her chest hurt. It had all been a lie. Every word. She pressed her fist between her breasts in an attempt to ease the pain.

"Did *you* kill Abner?" she hissed at Mr. Morris.

Startled by her accusation, Mr. Morris chuckled and shook his head. "You never told us Abner was killed, Rosie. You found him dead, you said. You brought his body to town, and we helped. I didn't need to kill your husband. All I had to do was wait for Abner to kill himself. Maybe *you* killed him. Did you wear him out?" Mr. Morris burst into a vulgar laugh. "Come on over to the bank. Be a good girl. An hour from now you can be fitted out in a brand new outfit with a pretty little bonnet and be headed out of this half-dead town for Tucson. No more eating cactus three times a day."

"I don't eat cactus!" Rosie screamed.

"Well, you look like you do," Mr. Morris yelled back, no longer laughing. "You can't work a gold claim by yourself. Don't be such a damned fool. Sell out. To me. That new so-called husband of yours won't be showing his face to you again. You can be sure of that. He was supposed to have you off that land inside of a week. He failed, so I fired him. He won't be getting any more pay from me. How much did *you* pay him? What was it he was supposed to do? Protect you?" Mr. Morris grinned, but it was an ugly smile. "Where is he now? Right where I found him. In a saloon. Drinking."

Rosie slapped the reins hard against Old Belle's and Faithful's bony backs and felt the two old horses leap ahead. She felt the goods in the buckboard shift dangerously. She felt the drag of Banjo still tied to the back… and then she forgot Del's horse as he came loose and trotted free.

Slowing, with dogged determination, she steered the buckboard around the plaza. She could hear Mr. Morris laughing. She nearly overturned before straightening out and aiming herself straight out of town.

She could hire all the husbands she could find, with or without conjugal rights, but it still wouldn't guarantee she wouldn't be alone for the rest of her life, Rosie told herself. Abner's land be damned!

She drove blindly ahead, feeling such pain she wished she were dead. She had fallen in love with Delmar Grant, and he had betrayed her from the very first.

• • •

In the musty darkness of the saloon, Del threw back a shot of whiskey and felt it scorch his throat. Wesley Morris had refused to take back the money he had paid Del in advance. Now Del was going to have to explain that to Rosie, too. No more putting it off.

If Del hadn't been married and in love, he would've shot Morris on the spot and been done with it. He could've ridden out of town, just as he had before when a job went bad. And what of it? He was a gunfighter. Men did not cross him. A part of him still felt like that reckless man he had been so short a time ago.

"Maybe you killed Rosie's husband," Del had accused.

Morris only laughed. "Abner Saladay was a stupid old man. He worked himself to death, prospecting. I've been out there myself. Of course, I have. There's nothing there. Not a damn thing."

"Then why do you still want the land? Why pay me to get Rosie off it? You like bullying helpless women?"

"You didn't ask that back when I hired you," Morris pointed out. "All you wanted was the cash money I could put in your whiskey-drinking, card-playing wastrel's hands. You're easy to buy. I know what's coming in this territory. Copper! I'd bet my last dollar there's copper on her land."

Del had no retort.

Downing another whiskey, Del knew he had to get to Rosie and try to explain. If she wanted that cactus patch and the ruins, he would to do everything he could to keep it for her. Wesley Morris be damned.

Del tossed a coin onto the saloon's bar. Somehow he would make Rosie understand. Outside, he heard the buckboard rattling past. Rosie lashed the horses and drove hell for leather out of sight.

She was leaving without him. Del made a useless dash

into the street. She was driving crazy fast. She would kill those poor horses. He saw Banjo trotting aimlessly not far away. He managed to catch hold of the halter. Banjo shied away.

"Hey, boy. It's okay," Del crooned. "Where's she off to in such a lather?"

Across the plaza, Del saw Wesley Morris and the storekeeper. By then Rosie had disappeared from sight. A terrible dread settled over Del's mind. Morris had told her. Del swallowed over a dry throat.

Throwing himself into the saddle, Del resisted the urge to hurry. He rode Banjo slowly around the plaza. He was going to kill that man. He understood the kind of man Wesley Morris was. He liked to win. Someday Arizona Territory would run big in mining. Morris wanted his share and didn't care who he hurt to get it. Del had worked for enough men like that to suddenly and completely despise himself for doing so. Men like his father and his brother.

Second class son.

Well, no more. Del was done with it.

Morris waited for Del with both hands resting on the pistols on his hips. Those twin pistols weren't for show. Del was no good to Rosie dead. Think, you damned fool. You put off telling her. Now you have to take your licks.

Riding in close as if he hadn't a care what was going on with Rosie, he asked, "What did you say to her?"

Morris gave Del a big grin. "None of your business, drifter. On your way."

Del stared him down. "I asked you a question."

Turning, Morris clicked his teeth out the side of his mouth, and strolled inside the general store. Seconds later he came out holding a shotgun loaded and aimed at Del's chest.

Del's heart stopped.

"If you're thinking about drawing on me, Grant, think twice. I told Rosie you were hired by me to get her off that land."

Dear God, put like that, Rosie would believe he betrayed her from the first.

It sounded like exactly what he had done.

But Del had pictured a stubborn, cantankerous old woman who needed his better judgment to get her off a desolate ranch to a better life. He pictured... his mother, needful of his help and protection. It hadn't seemed low down. Now he felt like the low-life scoundrel his father always believed him to be. Del had no right to feel angry. He felt sick. He'd been drunk. He had no excuse.

Staring down the shotgun barrel, Del wondered what he could say or do to convince Rosie that, from the instant he saw her, his purpose changed. His true intention had been to protect her from Wesley Morris himself and give back the advance. He just hadn't had the chance.

Morris watched Del, his eyes hard with the experience of successfully controlling anyone he wanted. "She didn't like hearing that," Wesley said casually. "Called you all kinds of unladylike names. Didn't she, Brummit? You didn't happen to take advantage of our little Rosie, did you, Grant?" He shook his head. "Shame on you. Lonely widow-lady like that, helpless out there in her cactus patch, grieving... I paid you to talk her off that land, but it looks like she's headed back that way. You didn't do your job, so get out of town. You're not wanted or needed around here anymore."

"You better leave Rosie alone," Del warned.

Morris shook his head. "It's only a matter of time. She'll come to her senses and drive back to town. To me. I'll get me that valley and whatever the hell she's hiding on it. I might even offer her more money, but I'll wear her down. You can count on it."

• • •

Lying snake! Rosie spit dust as it billowed into her face from the road.

Suddenly she had to slow the horses. She could see their sides heaving and was anguished to think she was driving them to death. Killing them would not ease the pain in her heart.

Grabbing her canteen, she climbed down from the buckboard's seat and rummaged in the buckboard to find the new bucket the clerk had loaded for her. She emptied the canteen into it and one by one, let the horses drink.

She would not cry, she thought. She was past tears. The sun burned her cheeks. Her new hat was gone. She didn't remember losing it. Her mind was in a tortuous whirl. How could he lie to her face like that, make love, and smile like it meant something?

She leaned against Faithful's heaving side and wondered what to do. Go back and shoot the bastard? She wanted to be home. She needed to get the horses to more water. She would have to unload everything herself and find something to eat. She was so God-awful rib-grinding hungry.

Feeling dizzy and overwhelmed, Rosie felt ready to scream out her frustration when she heard the approach of a galloping horse. Her lips tightened over her teeth. *Goddamn him.* Without looking, she knew it was Del. She should drive away and refuse to speak to him, she thought, but she couldn't make herself move. She wanted to see the look on his face. She wanted to hear his new lies. She would tell him to go straight to hell.

"Rosie!" Del yelled, slowing his horse and circling the buckboard.

His horse was heaving. There was a little water left in the bucket. Refusing to look at Del, she took it to Banjo.

"Rosie," Del said more softly, throwing himself off his horse and coming up to her, looming over her. "Let me explain."

"Explain how were you planning to get me off the land? Use me first, or did that idea come later? Kill me if I didn't go? Did you kill Abner, too?"

"Don't be crazy, Rosie," Del said with impatience. "I wasn't planning anything. From the first I wanted to help. Let me explain!"

She reached into her skirt pocket and pulled out the gun. *Kill him!* she thought. *He betrayed me. He never loved me.*

Del's eyes went wide but he didn't move.

"I'm sorry. I should've told you about Morris the first night, but I didn't know why the land was valuable. After that, it got harder and harder. I wanted to tell you. I planned to. I came to care about you. Love you. You've got to believe me."

Love? How could she resist those eyes? Didn't she know Del in a way she didn't know anybody else? Didn't she know he was telling the truth? Somehow?

She let the pistol drop. She was in love with a man who had betrayed her. It didn't matter what he had intended or when he had intended it.

"It's not just that," she said. "You didn't want to tell me where you came from. So what about your father, your brother, your house and land that is gone? Aren't you just dishonest by nature?"

His mouth hung open. It pulled down at the corners. Then he nodded just a little. "You're right. I've never been close to anybody. I don't know how to do it, same as you, Rosie."

That didn't seem fair. She wasn't going to be tricked again.

"You're fired, Mr. Grant," she said in her harshest tone. "Your services are no longer needed. If I see you at my ranch again, I'll shoot you dead. That's a promise."

She climbed back onto the buckboard.

Don't do it, Rosie. Don't ride away from him. If you go now, you'll be alone for the rest of your life. You love him. Forgive him. You were strangers when he made that deal and took money from Wesley Morris. Things changed after we were together. Things were good.

She remembered what she had felt only that morning when she woke in Del's arms. She had seen love in Del's eyes. She knew it. She knew Del, deep down, maybe better than he knew himself. But she couldn't risk it. She didn't trust herself. She tapped the lines against Old Belle's and Faithful's backs. "Git up," she said in a tremulous voice.

Don't look back.

The land was what was important, she reminded herself as she drove away. She must not abandon Abner's land. Abner died there. She was going to die there, too. Now she knew she would, and she accepted it. That was what her dream had meant.

Rosie watched heat rising off the hard scrabble ground

all around. She saw the saguaro cactus saluting her. She drove forward slowly, head high, listening for Del to call out something, plead with her, but she heard nothing. It had all been a lie, and now it was dead.

Nine

Del settled onto a hard chair facing Sheriff Aker's desk.
Hunger had become a dull ache in his belly. It was well past
noon, but he had no intention of eating. Rosie was foremost
in his mind. He had to do whatever he could to help her, and
to make things up to her.

"I'm trying to find out just what happened to Abner
Saladay," Del said to the sheriff.

Sheriff Aker had eyes like agates. He gazed balefully at
Del with a level of cynicism Del found irritating. "That so."

"When she brought her husband's body into town," Del
went on, "did she say where she found him and how he
died? Did you see Abner's body?"

The sheriff was long in answering. He looked at Del as
if trying to figure him out. "You married her, they tell me.
I was up to Tucson giving testimony at a trial at the time.
Why'd you do such a blame fool thing? Any female what
lives out on the desert by herself gets her brain dried up fast.
She told me Abner died in bed. She didn't look to be lying."

Del couldn't disguise his surprise. "In bed?" He couldn't believe it.

The sheriff gave Del a sly look. "You don't think he did? What's that crazy woman been telling you? He's dead. That's the thing. She got herself a new husband out of the deal. That's the end of it, far as I'm concerned. Too much woman for you, is she?"

Del bristled. "I want to know if you saw his body. Did it look like he died in bed or some other way?"

"Nothing special about his body, far as I could see. No reason for me to doubt her, even if she is crazy. You ask Doc Jeffers. He seen the body."

Del rose and nodded his thanks. He started for the door.

"Everything all right out at her place, Mr. Grant?" the sheriff asked. "I heard she left town a while ago... without you."

Feeling the hair rise on the back of his neck, Del turned and said, "She told me she found Abner outside... and she told me somebody killed him. I thought you might have noticed a wound, the marks of a fight, or something. I married her so I could work out there and protect her. Was he wearing night clothes?"

The sheriff grew thoughtful. He frowned, searching his memory. "Dusty is all," he said. "Dusty all over, shirt, trousers, suspenders..." He squinted at Del as if thinking pained his brain. "Oldest boots I ever seen on a man. Dirt in his hair. In his beard. Looked ninety years old if he was a day. Most pitiful excuse for a prospector I ever seen. Shame to waste a young woman on a man like that. You find any evidence to the contrary of what she told me, let me know. Now you mention it, he didn't look like he died in no bed, though lots of men sleep with their boots and clothes on."

"You know that Wesley Morris has been trying to buy Rosie's land," Del said as casually as he was able.

The sheriff nodded. "Yep, Wes has been trying ever since Rosie come from the east. Probably his way of keeping himself in the front of her mind. Every man in town wanted that little lady, still does, but she has proved damned unsociable. I know for a fact that day Rosie told me Abner died, Wesley was right here, playing poker with me and the boys at the miners' association. Get your facts 'fore you go around suggesting murder and mentioning names. Abner was loco for as long as I knew him. Ask him a question about his gold mine, he'd scurry away like a desert rat. If Rosie thought he was murdered, it was because that old fool planted the thought in her head."

Del wondered if that was all it was.

The sheriff leaned back in his chair. "Want to know what I think? Rosie Saladay played with your sympathies, boy. She needed a ranch hand willing to work for... what? Twenty a month? Who would work for that without feeling a little sympathy on the side? Not a man in this town. It took a stranger to fall for such a story. Murder." He sniffed a laugh. "She don't make enough money weaving them baskets of hers to keep a scorpion alive. I'll bet you didn't get nothing out of her except calluses and sunburn. Weren't no murder. Plain stupidness. That's all it was."

Del tipped his hat. "Thanks for the information, sheriff," he said and went out into the blazing sunshine.

He found his way to Dr. Raymond Jeffers's office. The man admitted him to a cramped room that smelled unpleasantly of strange medications. Del introduced himself and stated his reason for calling.

"I never treated Mr. Saladay for any serious malady," the doctor said, offering Del a chair. He was a thin man with an overlong beard. "Broken finger, years ago, but Rosie set that just fine, so he didn't need me for anything. When I examined the deceased, he appeared to be a malnourished man of advanced age who had been in bad health for an extended period. Rosie claimed he was fifty years old. He looked far older. I guessed him closer to seventy, so haggard was his appearance. His hands were battered from work. I saw no wounds, no scuffed knuckles, bruises, contusions or indications that he had been in any kind of fight. My assumption was he died of exhaustion. Why, may I ask, do you inquire about this so many weeks after the fact?"

"I'm not sure," Del admitted, feeling discouraged. "Sheriff Akers says Rosie told him Abner died in bed. I don't know why she would say that. She told me Abner died in an area where he had been working for years. Unfortunately, she and I have had a falling out. Before I move on, I have to satisfy myself that she is safe out there on her ranch land alone. She married me because she feared for her life. If she imagined that, I can understand. I'll move on only if I'm sure she's all right now."

"She was grief-stricken," the doctor offered. "Folks get disoriented in these parts. The heat and all. Women especially. Delicate creatures. No business out here in the desert."

"Exactly," Del said, "But if there is any chance someone is waiting to harm her, I can't leave until I see her safe."

The doctor shifted in his seat, and then with a crease deepening between his brows, he said, "Abner's left hand was in a claw." He demonstrated with his own hand so

Del would understand what he meant. "As if he had been reaching hard for something the moment he died. He might have suffered a stroke and been paralyzed. His expression was anguished. Not uncommon for a man dying in pain."

"The sheriff said his clothes were dusty," Del said.

"Ah, well, he was brought into town by buckboard, wasn't he? A dusty ride for anyone. But yes, he was covered in dirt. He was a prospector, after all. His clothes were nearly worn through. I doubt the man bathed." The doctor shook his head. "Abner Saladay was driven, you see. I see it in those deranged by gold fever. He lived in Diablo Rock almost ten years. I saw him only a handful of times. Keen eyes, abstracted countenance, totally fanatical in his pursuit."

"Out of his mind? Imagining enemies where there were none?" Del asked.

"Can't say, but that wouldn't surprise me," the doctor said. "You say Rosie plans to stay out there by herself now? A woman can't live in the desert without a man. She'll die out there."

"That's what I've been trying to tell her, Doctor."

"Won't listen to you?"

Del shook his head.

"Well then, what can a man do?"

After thanking the doctor, Del made his exit. He felt no better than he had when he first stepped into the sheriff's office. He corralled Banjo in the livery barn and fell on a meal at the restaurant. He scarcely tasted a bite. He took a room that night at the one saloon that had rooms for rent. It was time to figure out how he was going to save Rosie's life.

• • •

Feeling like a stranger to herself, Rosie walked into her ugly dirt-roofed house. She had been so happy that morning when they started for town. Now her life was in ruin.

There was a strange coolness inside the house. Everything seemed to be in place. Chipped plates were stacked on the dry sink. A straightened shelf held a variety of her smallest woven baskets. The table was clear but covered in desert dust. The floor felt gritty beneath her shoes.

The curtains covering the two bedroom doorways hung listless, reminding her of lovemaking she longed to forget. Even the fireplace made her think of Del, of how his face looked golden in the firelight, of how he looked carrying in loads of kindling with big capable hands.

Her heart turned over.

She wasn't reminded of Abner. It felt as if he had never lived here, as if he had ceased to exist. It was several seconds before Rosie remembered that there had ever been a bedraggled old man who used to totter into the house of an evening and sink to the stool in front of the table almost too exhausted to lift a spoonful of soup to his lips.

She stood looking around the room and wondered where her memories of Abner had gone. She could not recall anything he had said in those last few years. Oh, there had been conversation in the early years, but gradually that had dried up. Abner stopped sharing his discoveries with her. It was as if she had been working in the mill again, silent, numb, empty of thoughts, year after year, doing her job without a hope for tomorrow.

Delmar Grant had changed all that. He brought life back to this room, she thought. He had given her hope.

Crossing to the curtain that covered the doorway to

the room Del had made his own, Rosie could almost smell him there. Del's extra shirts hung from pegs on the wall. There was his bedroll. He had expected to come back, Rosie thought, feeling her throat tighten. Del had not been acting like a man guilty of lies and deception.

She twisted away and fled the house. Outside, she had to tend Old Belle and Faithful. They both looked very bad off because of the way she had driven them home. She felt awful and brought all the water and hay she could manage.

Everywhere she looked she saw evidence of Del's hard work. The sturdy corral fence. The cleared ground, free of dead clumps of grass and rough gravel. The barn itself stood straighter. The stalls were braced, the roof brush replenished. It was easier to get the bucket beneath the dribble of water at the spring. His shaving mug and straight razor were poised on a rock as if he would be back at any moment.

If he had been there, he would be hard at work unloading the buckboard. He would have the fodder under shelter where it would not dry out in the sun. He would have the food stores in the house, the lumber stacked and ready for assembling an irrigation system for her truck garden.

Her heart cried out to think he would not be coming back, that she had sent him away and vowed to shoot him if she ever saw him again. The thought was unbearable. Everything he had done here, for her, seemingly for free, she thought... he had done it all for Wesley Morris's money. She felt a sudden overwhelming urge to burn the house down. And the barn. But, shaking, she got herself back into the house where she lay down stiffly in her bed to cry.

No tears came.

She could see the sky through her new little window.

Fresh air wafted in reminding her of what it felt like to smile and laugh.

All the next day Rosie gathered long grasses she used for weaving… and watched for Del. As she tended the horses and fetched water, she listened for Del's horse. As the sun went beyond the western ridge, casting the entire valley into shadow that afternoon, and the cool night air descended all around her, she stood in the yard and stared at the place where she knew she would see Del if he came riding in. He didn't come.

She willed him to come.

Still, he didn't come.

Oh, she'd give him a piece of her mind when he got there, but she would let him put Banjo in the barn. She would admit him to the house. She would place a slice of ham on his plate—she had to eat the ham or it would go bad. He wouldn't leave her there alone, knowing how she felt about being alone. Del would come home.

And they would make love again…

She lay awake in bed a second night, waiting, listening, staring at the window. In her imagination they had already had their most terrible argument, made up and come together in her bed again.

Del didn't come.

Now her hopes, and the things she imagined she would say, dried up.

• • •

Del walked into Brummit's General Store.

"Looking for a new shirt?" Brummit asked as Del picked

through a stack of them. He scowled at Del openly.

"Getting ready to leave town," Del said off-handedly.

Brummit raised his brows. "Glad to hear it. Folks around here don't think much of you. I told Rosie she ought to annul that marriage with you. I'll see to it she's taken care of. Give her decent amount of time to mourn Abner… she'll be fine."

Del grabbed a blue shirt. "Mind if I change into this?"

"Back there." Brummit indicated a curtained back room.

After Del changed into his new shirt, he came out to wait while Brummit attended another customer who had just walked in. He tried on a new hat. Leaning on the counter, Del noticed a box of arrowheads on a shelf behind the cash box.

"This all for you today?" Brummit asked when he had seen his customer to the door and came back.

"That's a lot of arrowheads," Del said as casually as he was able.

"Folks find arrowheads around here any day of the week," Brummit said. His gaze was steady and cool.

"Do you know Wesley Morris well?" Del asked, trying on the hat.

Brummit smirked. "He's no favorite."

"Why is he so bent on getting Rosie off her land?" Del asked.

"Thinks he's going to be big with mining someday. I'm surprised Rosie stood up to him."

"What do you think Rosie should do about her land?"

"I don't give a tinker's damn about her land. She ought to move to town and leave mining to men. There's Apaches out there, rattlers, scorpions by the bucketful, bandits of every color and temperament. If Morris just left her alone, she'd be here right now, but no, he's got to push her. He thinks money buys anything." He shook his head. "Not a woman. You can't please a woman. Ask me. I know. I'll never understand females. I traded with Rosie all these years. Did she appreciate that? Did she come to me for help when she brought Abner's body to town? She acts like she has to do every damn thing herself." He moved the box of arrowheads under the counter.

Del watched the man.

"What do I think of Wesley Morris?" Brummit went on, warming to his subject. "I was a feature in this town long before Morris set foot here. Comes into my store full of stories about how he helped drive the Indians off the land. And then he looks at my wife. I should've shot him."

Del didn't like Brummit.

"My boys grew up and took off. Here I am. I'll be here after you're long gone."

"You ever been out to visit Rosie and Abner? I wondered what he was like."

Brummit shook his head. "Headed out of town today? Where to?"

"Tucson," Del said, giving the brim of the hat a tug down over his eyes.

"Have a good trip. Don't come back."

Del paid for his new shirt, hat and supplies. Brummit stood on his store's porch as Del rode slowly out of town. Wesley Morris was probably somewhere nearby, too, watching from a shadowed saloon doorway. Del slumped in his saddle as if he were discouraged and beaten. He kept his hands slack on the reins. But he was watching.

He knew what he was going to do.

Ten

Rosie heard the approach of a rider, threw aside the basket she was trying to weave with poor success, and dashed to the door.

The sun was high and blazing. It must've been past noon. Heat waves rose off the valley floor. Her feeling of vulnerability flared like a brush fire. She reached for her gun. Who would dare to come so far onto her property?

She couldn't make out who was riding toward her except it wasn't Del. Her heart sank. That wasn't Del's horse. In all the years she and Abner had lived there, only a few strangers had ever found their way through the rocky passageway into the valley from the road. A warning shout from the doorway, and her gun barrel jutting out, had always been enough to send a curious stranger away.

When the rider was within earshot, Rosie yelled from the doorway in her deepest voice, "You're on private property! Turn around and don't come back!"

The rider halted.

With her heart drumming, Rosie waited for the rider to turn his horse, but when he didn't, she cocked her gun.

"I got your head in my sights!" she yelled as forcefully as she could. "I'm a crack shot!" Her hands were shaking.

The rider kept coming.

Hoping she didn't have to make good her threat, Rosie sent a warning shot over the rider's head. The sound of it resounded across the valley and shocked her senses. She couldn't believe she had actually pulled the trigger.

"This is private property! Get out!" She was shaking all over now. She didn't want to have to kill a man. If nothing else, it would mean another trip to town with another dead body. "Get the hell off this land!" she yelled. "You're trespassing!"

"It's me, Rosie," she heard a man call. For a desperate moment she so wanted it to be Del's voice. Her heart leapt with hope.

But then she saw the darkly bearded face and realized it was Bear Brummit. She lowered the hammer of her gun. She didn't like him taking the liberty of coming all the way out to where she lived. This was just the kind of thing she had wanted to avoid by remarrying.

"What do you want, Mr. Brummit?" she snapped, stepping outside into the hot sunshine. She kept the gun at her side, well within sight, but she had to squint to see Mr. Brummit's face in the glare. "I might've shot you. You know Abner didn't want anybody coming here. I don't either."

Keeping a good ten yards' distance from her, Mr. Brummit reined and then climbed from his horse. He removed his hat. His slicked-back hair shone with oil. "Afternoon, Rosie. Was you expecting trouble?" He gave a nod toward the gun. He wasn't smiling.

"What do you want?"

"I come to pay a call is all," he said, looking peeved. His eyes swept over her. Then he looked around at the place. It looked a sight better than it had when she brought Del there the first time. "I thought you might want to know that hired husband of yours left town yesterday. Headed for Tucson, he said."

Rosie swallowed hard. "So you've told me. Go on back to town. I don't need anybody's help here. I'm fine alone, and I *will* shoot you if you come any closer!"

Rosie couldn't remember if she had ever seen Mr. Brummit smile before, but he did so now. Did he think she was joking? His smile was really no more a broadening of the space beneath his mustache. He was wearing what looked like a new shirt and suspenders. He reeked of bay rum.

"I ain't never seen the inside of your place," Mr. Brummit said in a pleasant tone. "Want to invite me in?"

"You've never seen this place at all, as far as I know," Rosie said. "Have you been out here before?"

"Why, sure, years ago, before you got here. I traded with Abner from the start. Now, don't act so skittish. I'm not here to harm you. Why would I harm you? It's a thirsty ride out here. Can't you be sociable and offer me a drink?"

She didn't want to reveal even the existence of water on her place, so she didn't point to the spring where he might fetch himself and his horse some water. She stared into Mr. Brummit's eyes, sick at the sight of him. His mouth might be attempting a smile, but his eyes were the same shrewd black as always.

"I didn't invite you here. I don't have drinking water in the house." She lifted the gun barrel a few inches. She would wing him first, she decided. Arm or leg?

He moved so fast, Rosie was startled from her thoughts. One minute she was looking at Mr. Brummit's eyes. The next he had her slammed up against the sun-warmed outside wall of her house. His hand gripped her wrist so hard she was sure he meant to break the bones.

"I mean you no harm, Rosie," he crooned through his teeth, pressing hard against her and looking down into her face.

She could smell his licorice-whip breath. She was taken so by surprise all she could think was that he must have bad teeth to disguise the smell of his breath with candy from his store.

"I've considered myself your friend a lot of years, Rosie. I've worried about you out here alone. Now, calm down and understand that I'm here to pay a friendly call on you. You were willing to *marry* a stranger and bring him out here. I say you owe *me* a little something for all the trading we done. I didn't have to take your baskets, you know. I helped you out when no one else bothered. Turn loose of your gun now. Drop it down onto the ground like a good girl. I didn't come out here to get shot at."

"Turn loose of my wrist," she hissed defiantly.

The moment he loosened his grip, she jammed the barrel of her gun into his side. She knew she was bruising him. She cocked the hammer.

"Get away from me," she said as harshly as she could. "You ever come here again, I'll shoot you on sight. Back off right now. If I pull the trigger, you're dead, and you know it. I'll swear out a complaint against you with the sheriff the next time I come to town. I swear I will! Go!"

Mr. Brummit's lower lip protruded as he frowned down at her in disbelief. His dark eyes glittered with malice. He didn't care about her, Rosie was certain. Like everyone else, he only wanted her land. Offering to marry her was just his way of trying to get it. She just wished he couldn't feel her trembling as he pressed so rudely against her. He knew she was afraid.

The instant the pressure of his body against her eased, she twisted away and flung herself into the house. The door was stout pine. She slammed it with all her strength. Dirt sifted down between the logs supporting the roof. The door might withstand a gunshot, but the window was so large Mr. Brummit could easily smash it and step inside.

Rosie couldn't move fast enough. She felt clumsy with fear as she lifted the pine log into the brackets that barred the door. Through the window, she could see Brummit standing in the yard, fuming.

Leaning against the door, she listened for some parting remark but he said nothing. A minute ticked by. He must be trying to decide what to do. Who would she trade with now, she wondered, feeling heartsick. She would never set foot in his store again.

Was that a sigh of exasperation she heard on the other side of the door? Then footsteps crunching, the creak of saddle leather. Rosie gasped for breath, fighting tears as she heard the first scuff of the horse's hooves moving away in the gravel.

Had she overreacted? Her hostility had driven Mr. Brummit to press his cause and reveal the kind of man he was. Now she had another enemy.

• • •

Del established a crude camp within a cluster of boulders among the rim rocks on the eastern ridge of Rosie's valley. It was a place sheltered enough that he could sleep a little without fear of being discovered.

He had spent much of the previous night riding along the ridge where he could see the faint light from her house. At dawn he had watched her emerge from the house and scan the valley before going to the barn and the spring. When she went back inside the house, and he was certain she would spend most of the day inside weaving, he felt safe in exploring near the box canyon.

He found a place where he could view the horse trail they had taken the day they visited the canyon. He supposed he was looking directly down upon the area where the ancient marking identified the opening to the canyon. From there he made his way deep among the boulders and wind-twisted pines on the mesa in hopes of glimpsing the brow of rock sheltering the cliff dwellings.

It was an arduous search done completely on foot. He left Banjo at his camp. He imagined ancient people traveling the same mesa. Perhaps ancient enemies had tried to find the hidden cliff dwellings. He wondered if someone had stumbled upon Abner at his work coming from this direction. But he saw no tracks. There was no indication whatsoever that anyone had passed that way in years.

It was late in the afternoon when Del struggled to find his way back to his camp where Banjo waited in the gloom. He was hungry, tired and frustrated. He felt he was wasting his time, searching, while Rosie lived on at the ranch house by herself. He wanted to be with her. He did not want to be there on the mesa in the heat, looking for something he was afraid he would never find, a second entrance to the ruins and proof Abner had been ambushed.

But then, just when he was reaching for dried jerky, he lifted his head. He smelled something on the wind, a scent that did not belong in the desert. He couldn't bring to mind what it was. On guard, Del climbed to the nearest high point and, keeping himself low to the rocks, turned his face into the breeze.

There was someone up there. He could hear his own heart thumping in his ears. It was possible someone had happened upon Abner this way. A demented old man might have reacted very badly to an unexpected visitor. It could have been Apaches. A prospector.

Del heard gravel dribbling down a steep trail. It sounded like the scrabble of climbing footsteps on rocks, a slip, a curse, heavy breathing, all on the wind. The sound could have carried from a mile away. Listening hard, Del held his breath.

White man, Del thought finally, his every sense on alert. Indians didn't smell like that.

He moved stealthily to where he thought the scent and sounds were coming from. He moved and then stopped to listen again. After a few seconds, he saw through the late afternoon haze, a rider disappearing around a jumble of boulders.

Del dashed to follow, but the rider vanished down a gulch. He must've been moving at a gallop there. Del heard distant hoof beats. There was no way of knowing which direction he had taken. Without Banjo close at hand there was no hope of following.

Retracing the man's tracks, he found where a horse had been tied for a time. Picking his way to a dangerous ledge of rock, Del saw not the well-hidden cliff dwellings themselves, but a dark corner of the deep box canyon. Even in the waning light, anyone happening upon a sight like this would be fascinated. One would want to find a way to climb down. Locating a water source in the desert was always a hope, as important as gold. Deep places suggested the possibility of cool retreat, and water.

Whoever had been climbing in this area, Del noted, was clumsy. The intruder left a trail even Del could follow. By the tracks along the top of the ridge, Del saw the first of several natural stone steps. Making his way down to the box canyon floor, he felt certain no casual intruder had happened this way. This was a known entrance to someone coming here regularly. This was what Del had been searching for all day. The second entrance to the ruins.

Had he explored the box canyon more thoroughly when he was there with Rosie, he might have found it. He should have visualized the long ago inhabitants going about their daily lives. He might have guessed there was a way out up this secluded corner. Standing in the shadow of the ridge Del could see across to the clearing where Abner once worked beneath his lean-to. Someone might have easily plundered the ruins without Abner ever noticing.

Del made his way up to the ruins on a precipitous slope of sliding gravel. He watched for any sort of disturbance in the stones or on a hard-packed footpath he reached that might indicate someone had walked there less than an hour before. In another hour the wind would cover any signs of a trespasser. Del hadn't studied Abner's journals closely enough to see if diagrams extended this far.

The question was, were these ruins even a secret at all? Torn as to what he should do, Del crept along the footpath skirting the high rock wall. He watched the gravel. He sniffed the air and listened with all his concentration. Then he saw the fallen wall ahead where the ancient rocks had been freshly broken. Their jagged, deeply colored edges revealed this was a recent collapse. It looked as if someone had purposely smashed through to gain entrance.

It was happening already, Del thought with a sinking heart. It was just as Abner Saladay had feared. Destruction of irreplaceable ruins had begun.

Angry over such wanton damage, Del climbed over the rubble, wondering when this harm had been done. It might have been only yesterday or months before. He saw boot prints in the dust, and his breath caught. They went into and out of the stone room on the far side of the fallen wall. The prints clearly showed in dust so old he couldn't hope to guess when the last ancient dweller had walked there. Whoever was coming there now had come several times. Within the last few days, Del thought.

In the adjoining stone-walled room he found the first signs of digging, a hole two feet wide and almost as deep. In the room beyond he found a shovel and several more hastily dug holes. Ancient pots recently smashed lay all around. Objects Abner Saladay would have meticulously unearthed, examined and recorded with professional reverence had been tossed aside.

Del bent and picked up a tiny blue shape lying in the dust. He was taken aback to realize it was a hand-carved bear, crude but recognizable. He wasn't sure of the mineral's name but it was exotically beautiful. Thin traces of brown patterned the blue rock. The hair rose on the back of Del's neck. What other treasures lay here? How many were missing now?

Del placed the tiny bear on one of several narrow ledges that protruded from the otherwise smooth adobe wall. Looking up at an opening in the ceiling directly above his head, Del realized the ledges might be used as steps. He had no time to climb up and explore.

It was almost dark now. He might fall. He wanted to cross the canyon and bolt for the rocky passageway that would take him to Rosie's house, but he couldn't abandon Banjo. His horse needed water.

Reluctantly, Del made his way back to the rock staircase and found it just as treacherous to climb up as it had sounded when he first heard the intruder climbing out of the canyon. He was panting as he topped the rim and looked back to see only darkness. A horse and rider might plunge to their death, riding too fast along here.

It took an hour to find his way back to his hidden camp and see to Banjo's needs. Del ate his barely palatable jerky and dry corn pone without tasting it; it was too risky to attempt a campfire. He felt surrounded by unknown dangers.

Although he longed to be on his way back to Rosie to tell her of the second entrance, there was no moon to ride by. He had to stay put. He slept eventually, but it was the troubled sleep of a man in love with a woman he feared would hate him forever.

• • •

The lumber Rosie would've used to build an irrigation trough to the garden looked like bed slats now, nailed across the window. Now no one could break through the window, but the inside of the house felt like a tomb. No light could get in. She wasn't sure she could live like that for long. Even so, she felt a bit more secure than she had when she had awakened that morning.

When she went outside to catch her breath and fetch a fresh bucket of water from the spring, she was startled by a mounted rider standing not ten feet from her door. She nearly dropped her bucket.

Wesley Morris sat on horseback, waiting as if he had been there for hours. She was so surprised, she wanted to cuss. Had she been hammering so loudly she failed to hear his approach? Now there was no time to run inside for the gun.

"Building something?" he asked, attempting to sound friendly.

He seemed so tall, so intimidating, Rosie hated him afresh.

"What are you doing here, Mr. Morris?" she snapped.

He didn't dismount. He just looked down at her. He appeared rather dusty, sweat-streaked and irritable. Then he clicked the side of his mouth against his teeth. He shook his head disparagingly and cast his gaze over the ugly house. Rosie's crudely fashioned windchimes clattered in the morning breeze.

With interest he walked his horse fully around the house and then over to the barn. Then he came back to where Rosie stood rooted, feeling stupid with surprise. She didn't know what to do. Wesley Morris looked very frightening indeed, seated on his tooled leather saddle, his gleaming black knee boots giving him something of a military air.

"I told Milt Brummit, and now I'm telling you, Wesley Morris. Get off my land!" Flapping her skirts, she spooked his horse.

The horse reared. Morris gave a shout of surprise and toppled sideways, nearly getting tangled in his stirrups. He landed hard on his back. Rosie was so surprised at what she had accomplished, she nearly laughed. He lay still several seconds.

Rosie clapped her hands over her mouth. Was he dead? She would not apologize.

Slowly, painfully, Mr. Morris lifted his head and scowled at her. "What the hell damn fool crazy thing did you do that for? My back's broke." Teeth gritted with pain, he hoisted himself onto one elbow. His fancy black shirt was covered in dust. His hat had flown off. Wincing, taking a swipe at a rock he had landed on, Mr. Morris struggled to his feet. He stomped his right foot back into his boot. He dusted his shirt.

He took a step toward her, grimaced in pain, and then lowered his head to glare into Rosie's eyes as if he meant to demolish her. He was wearing his twin pistols, and his arms were akimbo, as if he intended to draw on her. Had she been a man, she was certain she would've been gunned down.

Before Morris could think of what more to say, she backed away. She wasn't going to let another man pin her to the wall.

"Are you going to force yourself on me, too?" she yelled at the top of her voice. She felt crazy reckless. "You big greedy men, taking advantage of a woman alone. I'm not afraid of you! And I am not selling out to you. If you're thinking of killing me, do it. I'm tired of chasing you men off."

By the expressions that passed over Mr. Morris' face, Rosie supposed he was considering a number of ways to reply. He wondered who else had come there to bother her. He might be wondering where her husband was. He considered charming her, but that idea faded. Like Milt Brummit, Wesley Morris was left with nothing to say that would convince her to leave.

"I thought," he finally said, limping toward his horse, "that as long as you were in the market for husbands, and wore out one and drove off the other, I'd come out here and offer up my humble self. I was going to ask you to marry me, Rosie."

She was so astonished, she couldn't reply. She wanted to laugh, and shame him somehow, but she didn't know how to do it.

Mr. Morris caught the reins of his horse, got his boot into the stirrup and swung himself with effort into the saddle. He was injured, but how badly, Rosie couldn't guess. Surely she had injured his pride more than he would ever admit.

He walked his horse up to where she stood, shaking with fear of him, and studied her. He had forgotten to retrieve his hat. It was blowing away like a tumbleweed. She wasn't going to run after it. Without it, Wesley Morris looked rather ordinary, she thought. Why was she so afraid of a blowhard?

She met his eyes squarely.

"Come to think of it, you're not worth the trouble," he said. "It doesn't surprise me, now that I get a real up-close look at you, why Abner spent all his time prospecting. You looked dried up. And that young buck you snagged at

CACTUS ROSE

the saloon… what was his name? Del-mar? He didn't last long, did he? Worthless saddle tramp. Even he could see that there's nothing out here worth the taking." Wesley yanked the reins and turned his horse. "Dried up old dusty hag of a worthless woman," he muttered. "Thinks she's such a prize, living out here with the cactus and the scorpions. She doesn't give me the slightest tingle of interest. Be better off killing herself." He kept muttering as he rode slowly away. "Apaches wouldn't even want that."

Rosie's heart twisted. Mr. Morris was leaving, thank God, so that was all that mattered, but he left behind desolation in her heart.

· · ·

At dusk Rosie was still weepy when she heard yet another rider reining in at her barred door. She had the window covered and there was no fire in the hearth, no food on her table, no hope in her heart. When the first knock came, she didn't move from her bed. There was no fight left in her. If someone wanted the land, let them take it, she thought. She didn't care anymore.

"Rosie, are you in there? Are you all right?"

She heard a splintering crash as the door was busted out of its frame. Her body flooded with terror. She heard the table scrape aside. Dirt sifted down from between the log beams overhead as someone bumped hard into the center post in the main room. Then the curtain was torn aside.

Rosie bit back a scream.

"Rosie! Are you sick?" Del asked, falling on his knees at her bedside.

His eyes were wild with alarm. He searched her face for some kind of explanation. She was speechless with surprise. He grabbed her up and enfolded her in his arms. Rosie fell limp, powerless to resist him. She had needed him for days, and at last, at last he was there.

For a short wonderful moment she couldn't remember why she hated him so.

Eleven

Rosie struggled to free herself from Del's embrace.

"Let me go!" she gasped. "Get away. I want to get up!"

"Rosie, let me explain!" He looked so anguished.

"Oh, you're going to explain, all right. Get out there and light the lantern. I'm not having this out with you in the dark."

Del did as he was ordered.

Rosie tore her curtain aside. The stick that held it up come loose and fell on her head. Tangled in calico, she stomped into the main room and glared up at Del. Oh, it was so good to have him back. The door lay in pieces across the floor. He had kicked it loose from the frame. She felt startled to think how easily he had broken in.

"They told me you left town."

Del grabbed her arm. "Sit down, Rosie. Please." With a pout, she obeyed. "I told you I was never going to leave you. Even after you told me to go, I didn't go. Did I? I've been watching over you. Who told you I'd left town?" His

177

expression was like a thundercloud. "I need to know!"

"Milt Brummit. Wesley Morris," she snapped, spoiling for a fight. "They've both been here, thinking they could take your place. Never mind that. I don't want to know what you were hired to do. I just want to know why you didn't tell me before we…"

"You were hell-bent on getting married. I couldn't let you marry someone else. I didn't know anything about you except I had to protect you. Morris just said there was a widow on some land he wanted. Talk her into selling, he said. I thought, sure. I can help some old lady see reason. I intended she get a fair deal. I've hired on to do jobs I knew little about before I started. It always worked out… well, almost always. Things work out when the man doing the hiring isn't a thief. Morris was planning to pay good money, he claimed."

Rosie watched Del trying to explain. There was really only one thing she needed to know. Did he love her as much as she loved him? Did he love her enough to stay? She realized she already knew. She could see it in Del's crystal blue eyes.

"I never expected to fall in love with you, Rosie. I never expected that you'd find out—I tried to give back the advance. He threw the money on the ground, fired me. After that I figured I might as well take his money. I wasn't going to let it blow away—I could help you with it. I spent some looking after you. I brought more supplies."

Then he crouched in front of her. His expression grew serious. He took her hands in his.

"Rosie, listen to me. I've been at the ruins. I found the other way in. Abner was right. And you were right. Someone could have been there when Abner died. Someone has been there lately, digging. The destruction to the rock walls has already begun."

Oh, Abner, Rosie thought, her heart aching. All his research, for nothing. The years. The loneliness. It had been hopeless from the first. She wanted to cry. She had tried so hard to help Abner, and now this.

"I want to go back there tonight," Del said. "I want to catch whoever is going there. You still want to see justice done, don't you, for Abner's sake?"

Another night alone in the house? Rosie couldn't bear it. "No, Del! Don't leave me here another night. I can't stand it. I'll go with you." Rosie jumped to her feet and threw her arms around his neck. He felt so solid and strong in her arms. She wasn't going to let him go this time. She wasn't going to be a fool anymore.

Del held her and kissed her. He shushed her protests. They had been apart too long. There was just the warmth of his hands moving over her, and the excitement she felt as they retreated to her room.

There, they found bliss again. The lantern went on burning on the table in the other room and the smashed door admitted the cool desert night air. They were warm and safe in the darkness of Rosie's room.

Banjo waited outside, still saddled, all night. The wind blew steadily across the brush and cactus of Rosie's valley. In time, Rosie and Del slept peacefully as they had not slept in days. Rosie felt secure in Del's arms. Del had never felt so content. If someone was sneaking into the box canyon to dig by night, Del forgot all about it.

But in the morning when Rosie woke and remembered that Del had come back to her, she found her bed empty.

"Del?" she called, trying not to feel alarmed.

There was no answer.

After a brief, frantic search, she found Del outside some distance from the spring. She ran to him, almost sobbing with relief that he was still there.

"What are you doing out here?" she cried. "I thought you'd left me again!"

Del smiled up at her. "Aw, Rosie. I was looking through Abner's journals. I hid them out here. It seemed safer than inside the house." He tapped one as if to say he had found what he was looking for. "He did know of the other entrance, the rock stairway I found the other night. There's a diagram of it." He showed it to her. "There is so much here, Rosie! Even if the ruins are damaged, there will always be this record."

Del pushed the journal back beneath a broad flat rock and scuffed dust over everything with his boot as he stood. With a fistful of dry brush, he swept away footprints he had left while standing there.

Then he urged her back toward the barn. Before she understood what he was doing, Del had Banjo unloaded of the previous night's supplies. He was ready to ride out.

"But Del," Rosie cried, shocked to realize he was leaving her when she was begging him not to go.

"I'll fix the door before I—"

"I can fix the door myself!" she shouted. "I'm begging you not to go, Del. Please! What's the hurry? Let's just live here together. Forget the ruins! We could—but wait, Del! Don't leave me! Don't leave me again!" she warned. "We could block the entrances. We could—stop! Now you're acting like Abner! Now all you care about is the ruins, but I'm the one left here alone waiting. Didn't you hear what I told you last night? Milt Brummit was here. He felt free to threaten me because I was alone."

Del's expression took on a dark reckless quality that suddenly alarmed her. She had never seen him look like that. It was like, suddenly, she no longer knew him. Now she was afraid.

"Did he hurt you?" Del asked. He looked ready to commit murder.

Rosie wasn't sure she liked that look on Del. He might do anything. She took several steps back. There, she thought, there was the gunfighter she had married. Now his eyes looked ugly and dangerous.

"No, he didn't hurt me," she bit out, "but he would have if he... Wesley Morris was here, too," she added, wondering if that fact would make Del stay. "He asked me to marry him! Can you believe it? I really am going crazy here, Del. I've come to hate this place. Now you're ready to chase after... we don't even know who we're fighting! Can't you wait a few hours? Or take me with you! We can wait at the ruins together. Just don't keep leaving me!"

Del paused. "I thought you wanted me to find out who killed Abner. That's how you drew me into this mess. Now you don't care about the ruins anymore? Or him?"

"I wanted you to marry me so I wouldn't be alone!" she screamed. "I thought you understood what it was like for me here! Being alone. Nobody to turn to. No one to help me. No one to... care."

"I guess I don't understand," Del snapped. "If you don't really care about the ruins, or justice for your dead husband, and you can't stand being alone, why the hell don't you just sell this damned land? Move into town. Move anywhere. It makes no sense, Rosie! Staying here. I thought I was coming around to your cause, the land, the ruins, the value of its history. What kind of crazy fool are you to stay here in misery year after year? And now, when I want to help you, to make some sense of all this, you just want to hunker down like some damned scorpion under a rock. This isn't living, Rosie! It's living death! I don't want to crawl into this grave with you!"

Del's words rang in Rosie's ears. Put like that, she had no answer. That was exactly what she wanted to do, all right, hunker down in her dirt-roofed house and go on living like a hermit, chasing people away and... and... it sounded sick.

"Don't leave me," she whispered in desperation. It was all she could think of to say. "Please don't leave me here alone another night."

"Then get in your damned buckboard. If you're so afraid of being alone, Rosie, drive yourself into town. I thought I was onto something important. I thought you believed it was important, too. If you don't care who's plundering the ruins and may have killed Abner, then neither do I. Why should I? I've had enough of this place."

He faltered for a moment. He looked startled by his own words.

Rosie stared at him in disbelief. She felt herself caught in something she didn't understand.

Del felt as if he had lived a moment like this more times than he could count, a reckless, crazy situation where he couldn't think fast enough for what was happening. All he could do was get mad. All he could do was lash out. All he could do was walk away.

He loved Rosie, and yet he had had more than enough of her inexplicable, irrational fears. She had a chokehold on his heart. He had to get away from her. He went out the door. He heard her gasp of surprise. He faltered. Could he really go? This time for good?

He could.

And he did.

• • •

There Del went, riding slowly away the same direction that Milt Brummit and Wesley Morris had gone. Delmar Grant. So-called gunfighter. Paid protector. Hired husband. Riding away toward the high rock-walled passageway to the road and back to town and God knew where after that. Gone for good this time. There was no doubt this time. He would not be back. Rosie had given herself to him. She had let him, a stranger, into her heart, but that hadn't been enough to hold him. She had known the secret bliss she had so longed for… but it didn't last. Only loneliness lasted.

Twisting away from her tortured thoughts, Rosie jumped to her feet. She would repair the door. She could do that much. But after a half hour all she managed to do was prop it in place and nail a length of lumber across it so it wouldn't fall from its frame again. It was too heavy for her. She was a prisoner in her own home now. Crazy, she thought.

Rosie spent a long and restless night alone in her bed. Sometimes it seemed she was wide awake, remembering

Del's return and his kisses, but then it seemed more like a dream. She wasn't sure if he had really come back or if she had dreamed it. All she knew was that she was in a dark room hearing the same words over and over, words growing ever fainter, ever more heartrending, "Don't leave me!"

She woke the next morning feeling as if she couldn't catch her breath.

It was easy to tear out the nails and free the door. It nearly fell in on her as she eased it to one side and stepped out into the fresh morning air. Immediately she heard the sound of riders, several of them, in the distance. She couldn't tell where the sounds were coming from. She heard the sounds of hooves against gravel, and men talking in an eerie echo across the valley. Disoriented in the glare of morning sunlight, Rosie could even smell the stirred up dust the riders were leaving behind. She saw them then, figures framed in a sunlit haze, men riding the perimeter of her valley, boldly exploring!

Riders on Abner's land.

Rosie couldn't conceive of it. Abner was going to be furious, she thought in a panic. He would carry on for days about the importance of meticulous research. Even a single person setting foot in the ruin would mar the perfection of the place. He would look wild and desperate. She would feel so afraid, so helpless, so miserably inadequate to help or soothe him.

Without thinking, Rosie saddled Old Belle and threw herself onto the old mare's back. She galloped across the valley floor until she was reining at the head of a column of riders, eight men strong, armed and supplied for an extended trek. There was only one face she recognized.

There, smirking in a new hat, was Wesley Morris. Toothpick in the corner of his mouth. Pistols jutting on his hips. If they went much farther, Rosie thought, they would discover the handprint entrance to Abner's box canyon. All would be lost.

Why should she care? Hadn't she told Del she no longer cared? But something deep inside reared up. She did care. How could she not? This land was Abner's legacy. It was all that was left of him.

She locked eyes with Wesley Morris, but she realized too late that she was one crazy woman against eight armed men. Before she could think of a single threat, Mr. Morris walked his horse up to where she sat on Old Belle, reached out and pushed her off.

Rosie landed hard on the ground, startled and in pain, on her left hip. Gravel cut her palm as she struggled to get up. She was stunned speechless. How could he do such a thing? Her skirts had protected her from a cluster of pincushion cactus.

Old Belle shied and trotted away, leaving Rosie sprawled on the ground listening to Wesley's men chuckle nervously. Did they approve of Wesley roughing up a woman? Or didn't they care?

"Keep looking!" Mr. Morris ordered the men.

They turned their mounts and rode on, leaving Rosie alone on the ground, looking up at Mr. Morris.

He tore the toothpick from between his teeth and flung it away.

"I think you and Abner have been playing everybody in Diablo Rock for fools all these years," he yelled, glaring down on Rosie. All pretense of cordiality vanished from his face.

Rosie watched the raging man climb down from his horse. Mr. Morris had a dangerous look when he was like that. He had no more pity or patience for her. He came up and jerked her to her feet. Her shoulder burned when he pulled her arm.

"My men and I have been here long enough this morning to see there's no prospecting going on in this valley," he ground out between his teeth. "None!"

Frightened, wondering what had possessed her to ride into this fight without her gun, Rosie tried to jerk free. Mr. Morris wouldn't release her arm.

"Not a single hole," he said. "No sluice box. No mineshaft. You come into town. You buy lumber. You make folks think your new husband is working a claim—where is it?" Morris gave her a violent shake. "You nearly break my back driving me off. From what? From you? You're not worth my trouble. Now, I want to know what you're guarding here. Tell me, or I'm never offering another nickel for the place. You've made a fool of me long enough!"

"There's no gold mine," Rosie said tiredly. "I never said there was. Neither did Abner."

Was he going to beat the secret out of her? Was it worth getting killed to keep the cliff dwellings safe, she wondered. She didn't think so, but she could not bring herself to betray them just yet. She couldn't believe Wesley Morris would really hurt her.

"I seen Abner's hands!" Morris exclaimed in frustration. "He had the hands of a hard-rock miner, a prospector. He didn't get hands like that sitting around weaving baskets with you all the day long."

When she still didn't respond, Morris pushed her away.

"You're going to tell me," he warned quietly, menacingly. He stormed up to his horse and threw himself into the saddle.

Rosie watched him ride after his men, leaving her alone in the brush with tears of fright standing on her cheeks. She saw him pause and turn his horse in a circle while making a slashing motion in the air with his arm. By the time she caught Old Belle and got herself onto her back again, she could just make out the first curls of smoke rising from the barn.

Oh God, Rosie thought in anguish, had they let Faithful out first?

Rosie was riding hard back to the house when she crossed paths with Faithful galloping in panic past her, going the opposite direction. Rosie slowed before reaching the flame-engulfed barn. There was nothing to be done. It was already a total loss. All those hours, gathering the brush, climbing the ladder, getting the brush on to shade the horses. She had been too young then to know it was an impossible task. Mr. Morris's men tore up the corral fence and threw the posts into the fire, too. Everything Del had done for her was going up in smoke.

Halting, Rosie slid from Old Belle's back and gave her a slap, sending her galloping away. She couldn't risk going closer to the house. The men were riding around it, whooping like Apaches. She wondered if they would burn it, too. There was only one place to go. If Wesley Morris and his men kept on in the direction they were headed in their search of the valley, Rosie might be able to reach the entrance to the box canyon before being seen.

• • •

Del stumbled out of the saloon and leaned hard against a pine post. The plaza was dark at that hour except for a few lantern-lit saloon windows. The cool night air was a relief after the blazing heat of the day. Across the way, he could just make out the hulking silhouette of Brummit's General Store. The store was dark. So were the two upstairs windows.

"Rough up my wife, will you," Del muttered.

He attempted a step into the street but the ground seemed uneven. He remembered another man who liked to intimidate and rough up a woman, his father. He had trouble balancing. He pulled his gun, but he was too drunk to aim it, so he spent a full minute getting it back into the holster.

He made his way along the wooden walkways until he fell off one and lay in the dirt for a while, staring up at the star-studded sky. He might be near the restaurant. He smelled chili. It might be a good idea to turn in, he told himself. He'd had enough whiskey for one night. It was one of those black miserable times when all he could hear was his father's voice railing at him while his brother stood off by himself, aloof and superior because he had the luck of being born first.

But there had been that last night, that final climactic night when his brother had transformed before Del's seventeen-year-old eyes. No more was his brother, James Grant, the perfect dutiful son. The war was on, headed straight for them and their land. And James had joined up. On the Union side.

Del remembered his father's face, twisted with disbelief as he ordered James to stay home. "Let Del join up," his father said with contempt. "What does it matter if that useless whelp gets himself killed? You're staying here. You're staying!"

James had said a calm and simple no. The brother Del had admired all his life for his obedience and devotion looked like a changeling as the truth of his hate for their father dawned on his face.

Beside himself with rage, their father had gone into his study and come back with his pistol. Del could see it clearly in his mind's eye, the long oiled barrel, the heavy ivory handle, the flash from the shot and the blood suddenly staining his brother's shirtsleeve. The father he had tried so hard to make love him with all his stupid and contrary rebellion, was capable of shooting at his own firstborn son. Del had realized in that terrible moment his father had to be crazy.

James walked out of the house. Del hadn't even had time to rush forward to protect him. He ran after him. He called out, but James never turned. He disappeared into the darkness. "Get out of this house," Del remembered his father saying.

Then his father flung the oil lamp across the entry hall, setting the place ablaze. Their plantation house was a smoking ruin long before the Army of the Potomac marched through. Del was a soldier himself when he received word his father died of a fever a few months later.

No going back, Del thought. All gone. The orchards. The fields and crops. The barns and livestock. Gone.

He should never have taken that first drink with Morris. Always he resolved to never drink and gamble his money away again, but something always showed him up for what he really was: his father's disappointment.

Where was Rosie? He needed Rosie. She was out there at her place all by herself, in her dirt-pile of a house, nursing her crazy ideas… don't sell the land, Rosie. Oh, no, don't ever sell the land.

Sell the land, Rosie. Love me instead.

Now he cared about the land too, and those damned cliff dwellings, those ancient rock walls and strangely shaped arrowheads and artifacts that somebody somewhere would care about someday… now all Rosie wanted was to go on living in that house, eat dirt pie for supper every night, wash in a dribble of a spring like some damned desert rat.

Beautiful woman like that with such a sweet smile… crazy as a twice-dead gopher. Del tried to stand. No place to sleep in this dirt, he thought. It was getting in his ears. "Where are you, Wesley Morris, you bastard? Propose to my wife, will you? We're married, you know. Really married. And I saw her first. She's mine."

Only he had gone off from her, Del reminded himself. Gone off and left Rosie because all she wanted him for was to keep her company. To hole up in that dirt pile. Make her a window so she could hide in there and look out once in a while. The hell he would. It wasn't a life! Did she drive off Abner like that, saying, "Oh, stay with me! Stay with me, Abner! Don't leave me." But hold out on him, make him crazy with her moods and her fears. God damn, women were a trial. He couldn't even leave until the judge came back to town. Had to sign something to get a dee-vorce. Otherwise he'd never be free of her.

A terrible affliction, a crazy wife. What was he going to do—?

Del felt himself being jerked roughly to his feet.

"No sleeping in the street, mister. Go on now, or you'll be spending the night in jail."

"Looking for Wesley Morris…"

"He's gone," came the voice in the darkness. It sounded like Sheriff Akers. "Rode off with a bunch of men earlier today. Said he wouldn't be back until he'd had himself a bellyful of cactus stew. Go on, now. You've had enough for one night. Go right in there. They'll give you a room cheap."

Del let himself get pushed into a saloon. "I'm a wastrel," he said to the bartender who brought him a whiskey but demanded payment before setting down the glass. Del produced two bits. "My pa called me that when I was six years old because I couldn't do all my older brother could do. Why's a man say that to his own boy? I ask you."

"What did your pa want you to do?" the bartender asked.

Del threw back the whiskey, but he was too far gone to feel it burn down his throat. "He wanted me to be second best because that made my older brother look better."

Yep, that was exactly it.

It had never made sense, but that was the why of it. Del was smarter in every way than his brother, but that didn't set with what his father had wanted to believe.

"Well," the bartender said with an indifferent stare. "Looks like you're living up to your pa's expectations right fine."

Twelve

Rosie pulled the back of her thin calico skirt up over her head to protect herself from the burning sun. Crouching behind a cluster of saw-tooth cactus and scrubby brush several hundred feet from her dirt-roofed house, and feeling like a frightened child, she listened with all her concentration.

Was Mr. Morris coming back to find her, or was he going to leave her there while he destroyed her house, too? From time to time she could hear his men, but they seemed to be riding away now. The scuffing of hooves and a trace of voices in the distance made her jump with alarm. When she looked up, they were nowhere in sight. Sounds could carry so strangely in the desert valley, she knew. She longed to be under cover somewhere. For once, being alone was all she wanted.

Let them go away, she prayed. What was she going to do to save herself?

Did she dare go back to the house? She didn't think so. They might burn it down around her, or bring the heavy dirt roof down on her head. She remained huddled in a shallow spot that was closer to the entrance to the box canyon than the passageway leading out to the road to town. There seemed to be only one thing left to do, and only one way left to go. To the ruins.

By moving as stealthily as a mountain cat, Rosie eventually reached the edge of the valley. The sun was high, blazing down on her. She felt dizzy from the heat and so thirsty she couldn't think.

Suddenly she heard Mr. Morris's men, seemingly very close. She ducked down, almost flat, to the hot dry ground. Hoof beats reverberated through the ground beneath her hands and knees. More faint voices carried on the wind.

Rising up a little, Rosie could see the men making camp in some shade cast by a large formation of boulders a fair distance from her. Her heart sank. Beyond was the house looking so small and forlorn in the blinding noonday sunlight. Smoke still lifted from the ruins of the barn. She felt desolate, looking at it. Was life here ever going to be the same after this?

Driven by raging thirst, Rosie crept ever more carefully toward the jumble of boulders that marked the handprint entrance to the box canyon and the ruins within. If she was seen there, the handprint and the entrance would be revealed. All would be lost. The ruins would be found and plundered. She didn't even know any more if she should still try to protect the whereabouts of the canyon. Her life was at stake. Maybe she should give up and let the place be discovered. She had been defending Abner's land so long it was only by force of habit now that she kept moving and disguising her tracks as she went.

When she reached the entrance where the fallen brush covered the ancient handprint, she did her best to pull some of the debris in after herself. A skilled tracker would see the disturbed branches, of course, but Wesley Morris was no tracker. His men were surely just a handful of drifters gathered in the saloon or at the miners' association and promised a day's wage. All she could do, she reasoned, was try to hide in the canyon as long as possible. Eventually Morris would have to give up and go away. She hoped she would not starve to death in the meantime.

It became blessedly cool and shady as she edged into the narrow rock passageway. She let down her skirt that had been shielding her head from the sun, and paused a moment to catch her breath. She longed to cry, but what was the use in crying, she wondered. That's what Matron had always said when she dragged Rosie out from under a bed in the orphans' home. Rosie had been wanting to cry for so very long now. Perhaps for all her life.

With grim determination she made her way the last few yards to the opening in the rocks. She remembered the expression on Abner's face the day he first showed her the handprint and passageway. She remembered the wonder and terror she felt that first time she followed him. The box canyon was in full sun now, as it had been that day, as it almost always was. Its rocks and hollows stood aglow in golden sunlight, looking as beautiful and serene as any place Rosie had ever seen. Abner's heaven on earth.

There was no need to hide her tracks now. If Wesley Morris and his men got this far, her presence there would no longer matter. Sadness welled up in Rosie so overpowering she almost couldn't take another step. It was only a matter of time now, she thought. The ruins were going to be found. It was hopeless to think she could prevent it. No wonder Abner had been so desperate to record every detail of the place before it was too late. The ruins were vanishing before her eyes, soon to be lost for all time to the winds of fate.

When Rosie finally made it to the pool where the spring water flowed, she fell to her knees. Here was Abner's life-blood, the same water that appeared so briefly in the valley near his house—her house—again it spilled here in a slow but steady stream. She stuck her face into the coolness and drank deeply. She was nearly sick with thirst. She had left the house to chase after Morris in such a hurry she hadn't had time to eat or drink. She'd gone off without her hat. Her head throbbed. She felt disoriented. She couldn't remember suddenly why she was there. What did she need to do? She was dying, she thought.

Sprawled by the pool, her body badly overheated, Rosie stared stupidly across the canyon at the cliff dwellings' looming walls ablaze in full sunlight. How eerie they looked. How grand. Where was Abner working today, she wondered. He was never around when she brought him lunch. He wasn't working at his table, she noted. From where she lay, it looked as if the wind had blown down his canvas lean-to. He must be so tired, so hungry, she thought. She so longed to help him. When she finally felt rested, she struggled to her feet. Her legs felt weak as she made her way across the rough ground toward Abner's table.

"Abner?" she called softly so as not to startle him.

Feeling uneasy, Rosie looked around. Something was wrong. Everything looked different.

It looked as if Abner hadn't been there in a long while.

Had he gone to town without her? Didn't he ever worry about her or wonder how she was, waiting for him at the house, doing chores, and weaving for hours? Didn't he care anything about her at all? She didn't love him, surely, not the way she wished to, but she had come to care what happened to him. Did she mean so little to him in return?

There was something she should be doing, she thought, struggling to remember. Something wasn't right. Why was she there?

She righted Abner's stool and sat down. She had never felt quite so disoriented before. Abner must be working in the ruins today, she thought, closing her eyes. It might be good to sleep a while.

She hated the ruins, really, she thought, opening her eyes to look at them. There was something otherworldly about them, rising up like that so silent and yet so watchful. What were they thinking, staring down at her, those old rocks piled up? Did they know how much she hated being there, trapped by Abner's obsession?

But she had to stay because they needed her, those terrible old rocks. She didn't know what to do, but she had to stay. She dared not leave.

She couldn't leave.

With her head swimming, Rosie finally got to her feet again and started walking toward the ruins. Her heartbeat thudded loudly in her ears. Her face felt dry and hot. Her thoughts swirled.

"Abner?" she called out, reluctant to disturb him at his work.

Sometimes when she came upon Abner working he would give a violent start. He would turn and look at her with such a blank expression. He would blink, as if he were bringing himself back from far away. He usually had a small brush in his hand, sometimes a tiny pick. Always there would be some fragile precious scrap of something half exposed in the soil. His journal would be nearby, a pale pencil sketch in progress that he would ink over under the shade of the lean-to later. He would make notes, take measurements, record the date and time. She would look at the half-buried artifact and feel a glimmer of interest, but usually her interest faded quickly. This was too much for one man, she always thought. It had always been much too much for her.

The area where the fallen cliff dwelling wall had once stood, rising solid to the top of the bluff, was now a jagged gaping hole, exposing a second and third floor and fragile, rotting timbers Rosie didn't remember seeing before. Below the shadowed hole was a heap of freshly fallen rubble, dusty broken adobe brick and shattered timbers.

A part of the ruin had fallen, Rosie realized, climbing closer. When had this happened? Abner must've been so terribly—

Rosie shook her head suddenly.

She stopped and pressed her trembling hands to her hot cheeks. Strands of her hair were still damp from drinking in the pool. Abner didn't know about this fallen wall, she thought, her thoughts clearing. Abner was dead. She had seen him buried in the fenced cemetery in Diablo Rock. Wesley Morris had walked up to her afterward and offered to buy the house and the land...

Dead.

He had been dead... weeks? This wasn't any ordinary afternoon. She wasn't bringing him lunch. Abner wasn't here.

She felt afraid, remembering. How could she have forgotten something like that? How could she have forgotten she was alone?

Del told her someone was plundering the ruins. Here was proof. The fallen wall. Abner's greatest fear was coming true. He had entrusted the ruins to her, and here she was failing him. She wanted to leave. She yearned to leave. She wished she never had to see the ruins again.

She heard a sound and whirled around to scan the box canyon with panic gripping her throat. She saw nothing moving, but there was someone in the canyon! She could feel it. Shrinking back against the rocks, she stood poised, listening.

From where she crouched, Rosie could see the entire box canyon from the rocky entrance that opened from the valley to the spring-water pool. The sky overhead was brilliant blue, so pure it hurt her eyes. The surrounding rocks, golden and brown and red in layers and strata, had been carved by time into this place of mystery. To her right the hulking boulders of the canyon wall were so immense no one could hope to climb them. For a moment it seemed like the rocks were gigantic elders, grouped together in judgment of her. She wished she could hide from them.

But she heard sounds again and something that might have been moaning. Footsteps. Was it Abner? She shook herself. Abner was dead. She didn't like feeling crazy like this. It was time to stop this nonsense.

Suddenly the darkness of one of those stone rooms seemed like a safer place to be than where she was, exposed at the base of the towering rock wall with its newly gaping wound. She remembered being there with Del.

She remembered how afraid she had been to step inside the ruins where the rocks seemed to speak to her of far-gone times and unknown lives. There had been no holes dug in the floor then. Entering the nearest doorway, Rosie stumbled to keep from stepping into one. All around was the rubble of broken pots and dirt piled up. Who would dig here so carelessly, Rosie wondered. Abner would have been beside himself.

An inner wall was down, too, leaving a space large enough for her to step cautiously through. In the adjoining rock-walled room was another hole dug in the floor, another rock wall knocked partially down. Her sense of sorrow became overwhelming. It was one thing to meticulously unearth the treasure of an ancient place, but to gouge it out with a shovel, to smash down walls, having no regard for...

She heard something again.

She scrambled to hide in a dark corner. Her fear was overwhelming now. Rosie saw shallow stone steps in the back wall of the room, leading up to a hole giving access to the next level above. She couldn't remember if Abner had ever spoken of exploring the upper rooms. She would be safe up there. She hated to climb up the steps; there was so little to hold on to. She might fall back and get hurt. She had already been pushed from her horse. Her bruised hip ached.

But she must keep herself safe. There was no one to help her. She had to wait for her head to clear. Then she would know what to do. She was overreacting. In time she would regain her senses and go back to her house, she told herself. She would rebuild.

Hiking her skirts up, Rosie made her way, stone by stone, up to a second level where the floor was made from ancient pine logs partially covered with crumbling adobe. The room was full of baskets. She wondered if Abner had put them there. It almost felt as if she were walking onto the roof of her house, but it felt none too sturdy. The timbers were old. Centuries old. Waiting a moment, Rosie listened. She heard something, someone, moving with difficulty not far away.

There were more shallow stone steps in the side wall. She climbed up and up again. In the third level she crawled along the edge of the rock-walled room where she hoped the floor was still sound. She found her way into an adjoining back room through a low narrow doorway. This room, deep within the third level of the cliff dwellings, had a rear wall of solid rock in a swirling pattern of colors. Drawing her skirts around her trembling legs, Rosie settled herself into a dim corner. It felt good to stop moving. It was cooler there. The wind sent a calming breeze all through the structure. The ceiling was a curve of stone so immense it was like being inside a mountain.

There was a small opening in the outer wall of the previous room, admitting a thin ribbon of sunlight. Rosie breathed in the dry air. She felt herself growing calmer. No one would find her there. And she wouldn't leave. She had promised she wouldn't leave. She wasn't going to go back on her promise no matter how much she wanted to.

• • •

Riding into the valley from the road, Del smelled the strong odor of wood smoke in the air. Immediately on the alert, he thought Rosie must be in the house, cooking. But the odor was too strong.

Desperate to see her again, and with his head aching with a hangover, he urged Banjo to a trot. The movement jarred his throbbing brain, but the thought of coming back for Rosie was worth the pain. When he rounded a low hill and saw the smoke rising from the ashes of the barn, his heart stopped. He heeled Banjo into a gallop.

There was no smoke rising from the house chimney. The doorway to the house stood gaping open, broken down as he had left it. The place had a haunting silence about it.

There were so many horse tracks around the house Del couldn't tell how many riders had been there, circling the place. He wasn't fooled. Those weren't Apache tracks. Thanks to the blowing wind, the tracks might have been made an hour ago, or yesterday. The corral fence had been torn up and burned, too. Who would have done that? Del was baffled. He saw no sign of Rosie's two horses. The buckboard was gone, too.

For a horrified moment Del wondered if Rosie had burned down her barn and abandoned the place. "Rosie!" he yelled, throwing himself to the ground. He staggered as he landed, disgusted with himself for getting drunk the night before. What good had that done? He was done with that for good and all.

The house was empty, the smashed door fallen to one side inside. She had boarded up the window. Who had she been defending against? The table was overturned. The lantern was smashed. Lamp oil had soaked into the stone floor. The curtains had been torn from both doorways, the contents of both trunks thrown around. This was not how she would have left the place.

He fixed his gaze on her work area. She'd been weaving…

baskets were piled in the corner. Therefore she had not gone to town to trade. She would've taken the baskets if she had.

There was her bonnet, her hat, her jacket… He felt sick with worry.

He looked into Rosie's room. His heart rolled over. How could he have ever been so angry he would leave her? What had happened to her? Where was she?

Outside, he tried to make sense of the tracks around the house. Who had terrorized Rosie? Had she been taken? Or was she driving the buckboard, fleeing somewhere? He was about to ride for the nearest high point where he might see most of the valley when he decided instead to follow the buckboard's wheel marks.

On foot, leading Banjo, Del moved as quickly as he could. The wheel marks were marred by numerous horse tracks. The riders must have been following her, he thought, not chasing her. Galloping horses would have left a different kind of trail.

The wheel marks were not out of control. They led, puzzlingly, away from the house toward the south. If Rosie was driving, she wasn't headed for the passageway to the road or toward the secret entrance to the box canyon marked by the handprint. "Rosie!" he called, hearing his voice echo across the valley. "ROSIE!"

The buckboard's wheel marks led in a meandering path toward the edge of the valley. Then they halted at the remains of a hasty campsite. Riders had burned Rosie's barn, circled the house like Indians, and then rode here and made camp? It didn't make sense.

A half dozen horses, perhaps, had been tied to a picket line here. He could see that marked in the dirt. The men had slept over there. Bedroll depressions, boot prints. Stepping cautiously to examine the signs, Del looked for something, anything, left behind to help him identify the intruders. The campfire was warm but then almost everything in the desert was warmed by the sun at that hour and would give off warmth for a while into the night. There was no time to search more thoroughly. The sun would be past the ridge soon. Darkness would fall. He had to find her.

• • •

It was nearly dark when Rosie woke with a start. Surrounded by shadows, she didn't remember where she was. She knew only that the smell of rock was all around her, a smell that seemed as familiar as her own bedroom.

Feeling around, she found a rough rock wall to one side and a crumbling adobe wall to the other side. There was a dirt floor beneath her. Her legs were tangled in her skirts. Disoriented, she scrambled to her feet in complete panic. Her first thought was that she had fallen into Abner's grave! This was what she had seen in her dream.

She ran a few steps toward the only light she could glimpse, and the floor gave way beneath her feet.

• • •

Del found Rosie's buckboard abandoned near the campsite, a wheel off. Mystified, Del followed the horse tracks leading away from it—it looked like eight horses—until he realized he had, indeed, failed to see their tracks exiting the valley by way of the road when he rode into the valley an hour ago. The intruders were gone.

Was Rosie with them? He wanted to ride back to the road, all the way to town if need be, but dared not kill Banjo by riding too fast. He had just come from town. He hadn't met anyone on the road. If Rosie was in town, she was safe enough. Del stood a long moment, waiting for his heart to slow, wondering if there was any chance she might still be in the valley. Hiding.

Doggedly, Del rode back to Rosie's house. He watered Banjo and took another—more careful—look around. He reassured himself that no one had plundered the places where he had hidden Abner's artifacts and journals. That, at least, had been one thing he did right. His time in the war had taught him to anticipate an enemy and be ready.

Then, feeling renewed energy, he set out for the box canyon. Rosie might be anywhere, but if she was in the box canyon she needed his help.

By the time he reached the handprint entrance, darkness had fallen. He almost missed the entrance, it was covered so well.

Before moving the branches to admit himself and Banjo into the passageway, he stood a long moment watching and listening. His sense of dread had eased. There wasn't much he would be able to do in the darkness, he knew. And neither could anyone else, luckily. He needed to find shelter. He was hungry and tired, but that didn't matter. At least he was sober.

Leading Banjo into the darkness of the looming rock entrance, Del moved with care until he emerged in the box canyon. It was utter blackness there. He dared not take another step. But he could smell the water in the tiny pool not far away, and so could Banjo. He let Banjo lead the way.

· · ·

Lying on her back in utter darkness, Rosie took stock of herself and knew that she had not been injured in the fall. Not seriously. There was no use panicking. It was dark, but she had known darkness for years. She could endure darkness a while.

She lay atop what felt like a heap of broken logs. Around her was the smell of ancient dirt and rock. Above her was darkness with a hint of a breeze. She supposed she could cry, but there was no use in it. She wanted to climb to her feet and leave, but the slightest movement might bring something more crashing down.

It grew cool. There was no way to know if she was surrounded by scorpions or rattlesnakes. Only the light of morning would tell. She let her breath out and lay still like she always did when she was trapped in circumstances beyond her control. In a short while she was able to sleep.

· · ·

Rosie woke to the sound of digging and quiet cursing.

Startled, she jumped and felt the rubble of broken logs beneath her shift alarmingly. She had to hold herself very still again. It was just dawn. The rock-walled chamber where she lay had filled with pearly light. Above her was a ragged hole edged with jagged timbers and broken adobe where she had fallen through. She could not tell if she was lying in a room on the first level or in a chamber below it. She didn't know if there was more chance of falling.

Whoever was in the ruins, digging, she thought, he was not far away. Rosie believed she could call out and be heard, but she wasn't sure it was wise to do so. She didn't feel panic. Whoever was in the ruins, digging, was an enemy of the ruins, and therefore an enemy to her. She must be careful.

She lay very still, feeling all her clarity of mind restored. She was in danger, but she wasn't helpless. She wiggled her shoulders and then her hips. The broken logs beneath her shifted. The hole in the ceiling was far enough above her that she would need help climbing out of this place. With exquisite care, she began to sit up. Debris shifted a little more beneath her, but she did not feel as if anything was going to give way.

Looking around, Rosie realized there were no openings in the room except the hole above her. The corners of the room were concealed by darkness. There were no doors, no window openings. Around the edges of the rock walls were baskets and pots covered in ancient dust. She was able to edge herself off the timbers where she had slept all night. Her back was sore, and she was a little stiff, but she was all right. With care she managed to stand. Some of the timbers shifted, making a slight noise. Above, not far away, the sounds of digging halted.

Rosie held herself very still. Her heart pattered with apprehension. After a moment, she looked in a nearby basket and wondered what had once been in it. Some kind of grain? This seemed to be a storeroom. There had to be a doorway, she thought. Ancient people would not have stored grain in a room with no access.

She heard softly crunching footsteps overhead.

Edging back into a dark corner toward what she sensed was the front of the stone-walled room, Rosie wondered suddenly why she didn't feel terrified. Whoever was up there had surely caused Abner's death, she thought, but... but why kill Abner? Was she wrong all this time? Had it been only an accident? Why would the plunderer want to kill Abner... or her? There was little Abner could have done to stop people from digging in the ruins. There was nothing she could do about it now. She realized her battle was at an end.

To be saved, Rosie thought, all she had to do was call out.

Thirteen

Where was the fear she had lived with all her life, Rosie wondered. She had lain all night in that rock chamber. It had been so dark she hadn't been able to see her hand in front of her face. She had been completely alone. She might have died there. No one would have known where to find her.

And yet she had kept her head. She had been able to wait. She had gone to sleep as if she were in her own bed. Well, almost. In that terrible darkness she had not been afraid.

What had happened to her during the night, Rosie wondered. She felt different.

Huddled in the corner, deciding what she was going to do, Rosie realized she had dreamed again. All the long night in the darkness she had dreamed of the last six years alone in her bed at the adobe ranch house while Abner snored softly in the other room. She dreamed of the mill where she worked as a girl, risking her hands and her life every day as she worked among the churning machines. She dreamed of the rows of beds in the orphans' home where she lay awake in such loneliness for so long.

And then in that long meandering dream came the darkness of that terrible night when her parents lay dying in their beds and she was so small.

Lying there in the ruins, Rosie hadn't shrunk from the memory. If she must think about it, she must. There was nothing else she could do there. She had reached the end of her sad journey. She had expected to be dead by morning.

When her parents died, they had been living in a tenement back east. She couldn't remember if they had candles or some kind of lamp. All she remembered was the bed and her parents lying there.

Her father had already died. She could feel the grasp of her mother's cool fingers, clutching her hand.

"Don't leave me, Rosie," her mother had whispered.

Rosie wouldn't have left her mother. But in time someone came and took her away. She grew up and worked at the mill. She answered Abner's ad. She rode all the way to Tucson by herself.

To do all that, Rosie thought, she had needed no great leap of courage. The nagging apprehension she had lived with all her life belonged to that childhood memory. Not to the here and now.

Rosie opened her eyes. It was all right to survive, she told herself. It was all right to go on without Abner. And these cliff dwellings? They had stood for centuries. They did not need her.

Fear hadn't brought her to this place in the ruins, Rosie thought. Courage had brought her. Courage and the desire to live had enabled her to endure. She was stronger than she had ever given herself credit for. Rosie felt so startled to discover her own courage, she forgot to be cautious. She took a step forward, disturbing some rubble. The sound was loud in the stony silence.

Slow, crunching footsteps on the level above came closer.

Drawing back, Rosie saw the shadow of a man lean toward the hole in the floor above. The man's face was too dark to recognize. Before she could call out to him for help, she saw the glint of morning light reflect on a pistol barrel. Seconds later, a deafening shot reverberated in the rock chamber. The bullet dug into the wall only a yard from Rosie's head.

Rosie screamed in surprise. "Don't shoot me!"

"Who's down there?" came a man's wild cry of alarm.

"It's me!" Rosie cried. "I'm trapped down here. Help me!"

There was a long pause of silence as the intruder considered what to do. Rosie held her breath.

She watched the shadowed man back away out of her line of sight.

Rosie dared not cry out for help a second time. He didn't intend to help her. She edged further into shadow. Who would shoot into the darkness before knowing what—or who—was there? She backed against the rough stone wall. There she saw the darkest corner of the room across from her, a low rock-lined tunnel leading out of the storage chamber toward a glimmer of dawn light. She would not have seen it if she hadn't been pressed so far into the darkness herself.

When she heard sudden running footsteps overhead, Rosie knew the intruder was getting away.

One look at the dark opening of the tunnel, and Rosie

knew she would have to risk going through it. She hoped this was the last test of her courage because she'd had just about enough of this horrible place. She stooped into the low tunnel that went for some ten feet at a crouch before emerging behind a boulder in the dim light of dawn. There, some fifteen feet away, she saw Milt Brummit standing in the pale dawn light, holding his gun while trying to scramble frantically up what looked like a natural stairway of boulders and stones to the top of the bluff.

His boot slipped. He tumbled backwards with a startled yell, landing hard on his back only a short distance from where Rosie had emerged from the ruin.

"Mr. Brummit?"

He tried to aim his gun at her but the pain in his back stopped him. He gave a groan of anguish. That gave Rosie enough time to rush at him and kick the gun from his hand. He yelled and put his stinging fingers to his mouth.

"What're you doing here?" she demanded, explosive with anger. "What are you taking from this place? You killed Abner, didn't you?" Her voice echoed across the canyon.

Brummit shook his head. "I didn't do anything to him! He—he came at *me*! He almost killed me, Rosie! Crazy ol' coot! Help me, Rosie. My back's broken."

"Your back's not broken," Rosie snapped, her patience gone. "What happened with Abner then? Why didn't you tell me what happened to him? Why keep coming here and stealing from this place? This is a special place. Are you so stupid you can't see that?"

Brummit closed his eyes, his face wretched with pain. He kept shaking his head back and forth. Then he struggled to sit up. He seemed to be taking his time. Immediately Rosie was suspicious. He wasn't badly injured by the fall. He was playing her for time.

She saw him glance around for the gun. She scrambled past him to grab it up. She was just turning it on him when they both heard a shout from across the canyon. Rosie turned to see Del riding Banjo toward them, waving his hat. Rosie was so surprised, so delighted and relieved, she couldn't believe he was actually there. She had thought him gone for good.

"Rosie!" Del shouted, reining hard a few feet away. "Are you all right?"

Brummit lunged at her.

She kicked away his grasping hand. Slipping in the gravel to avoid his clutching grasp, she managed to climb back to her feet. She wanted to pummel him.

Recklessly, Del threw himself from his horse. He caught Rosie in his arms and swung her around. "I didn't know where you were!" he yelled, panting. "I spent the night in the dark right over there. It was too dark to search for you. How did you get here? Where did you come from?"

"I was in there," she said, pointing to the ruins. She felt proud of herself for surviving the night. "In a deep place. All alone. On a pile of broken timber. All night, Del! And I wasn't afraid. Well, maybe a little." She gave him a small smile and then she laughed.

She turned her attention back to Brummit.

"Mr. Brummit," she said in a forceful tone. "Tell us what has been going on here." If he didn't tell her, she was going to wing him with his own gun, she decided. She took his gun and aimed it at him.

"I've been coming here for years," he said with scorn.

"There's gold here and I intend to find it. Morris is always talking about how there's a mine here. I wanted my share."

"There is no mine," Rosie exclaimed with exasperation. "Why won't anybody believe that? This place is the treasure!"

"This rock pile? You're crazy as Abner. He caught me here. That day he died. He came at me—I didn't know he didn't have a gun. I thought he was going to shoot me. He started yelling at me, acting crazy. He started hitting me. I hit him back. He was like a bag of dust. I drew on him, sure, but I didn't shoot him. I swear it. You know he wasn't shot, Rosie. Then he looked like he was pitching some kind of fit. Yelling about desecration and looting and… and… posterity. I didn't wait to see what he was going to do next. I—I got the hell out of here. I went back to town. Then the next day you came into town with his body…" Looking baffled, he stopped talking and looked away. "Damn ol' coot."

"You didn't think you might have killed him?" Rosie demanded to know.

"I didn't kill him," Brummit yelled back, glaring at her. "He was still ranting when I left. If I hadn't gotten out of here he would've killed me with his bare hands. He was crazy as a twice-dead gopher. What happened to him after I left, I don't know. And I don't care. He should've been locked up somewhere years ago."

"You took a handful of his arrowheads," Del said, giving Milt a look of disgust. "You're just a petty thief."

Brummit glared at him. "So what if I did? We argued, but I meant Abner no harm. He was alive when I left. I swear it!" He climbed to his feet and took a step away from them, wincing.

Seeing that Rosie and Del were more interested in

holding each other than doing anything to him, Brummit started scrambling up the rock stairway. He climbed with effort, tottering at one point so that Rosie feared he might fall to his death this time, but he made it to the top and disappeared. They could hear him limping away. Then there came the distant sound of hoof beats.

Rosie wilted into Del's arms. "Do you believe him?"

"Do you?" Del asked.

"Yes," she whispered. "Are you all right?" She handed him Brummit's gun. He stuck it into his waistband.

"Me? I'm fine!" Del laughed. "Rosie, I've been everywhere, looking for you. What happened? Do you know the barn burned down?"

She nodded.

Beginning to tell her story of the past many hours, she and Del made their way across the canyon floor back to the pool where they could drink and sit and rest. Rosie told Del about her reckless encounter with Wesley Morris and his men. Then she curled into his arms and relished the feel of him.

"We'll talk to the sheriff," she said when her story was done. "We'll find out what can be done… about *Mister* Morris… and *Mister* Brummit."

They sat a long time, pondering the cliff dwellings in silence. Del held her snuggly against his chest. She fit there so naturally it seemed as if she had always been with him.

Suddenly she drew back and looked at him in surprise. She had just remembered their last parting, and their final argument. She had thought she would never see him again. "You came back!"

"I should never have left," he said. "I love you."

"I should never have let you go," she said, planting a kiss on his cheek. "I was so confused. I was in the grip of something I didn't understand. Forgive me?"

Del chuckled. "Of course. What do you want to do now?"

"I want to eat," she said. "I haven't eaten in what seems like days. Did they burn the house, too?"

He shook his head. "They ransacked the place, but it's still standing."

"I suppose that's a good thing. I need a bath, too. I have the dirt of ages on me. Then I want to sleep in my own bed again." She kissed him tenderly. "With you."

• • •

With the broken pine door and nine-light window barred against any further unwelcome intruders, and a fire burning low in the fireplace, Del and Rosie cleaned up after their misadventures in a playful way that involved a washtub, lots of water and laughter. They ate a simple meal. Then they sat and talked of all that had happened, but all they really wanted was to lie down together.

At first they slept. They were both bone-tired. When Rosie woke in the night to feel the warmth of Del's body pressed close to her, she lay for a long time savoring the pleasure of it. She had never known such happiness. Not like this. Not with the hope of new tomorrows beckoning.

She listened to Del's soft breathing and marveled to think he had done so much to help her. He had changed her life. He had awakened her. Saved her.

And, all that night when she thought she was alone in

the fallen part of the ruin, Del had been across the canyon, waiting for dawn in order to find her. Now she lay in the darkness of her own familiar room, safe, breathing in the fresh air flowing in from that ragged window that had no glass or curtain. How wonderful everything seemed. Nothing would ever be the same again, she thought, and that was good. The old frightened, desperate Rosie had died sometime during the past few days. In her place was a new woman born. If the old Rosie had been crazy and reckless to ride into town to hire herself a husband that day so short a time ago, it had been a much needed craziness in her empty life.

Del stirred beside her. It felt as if he was surprised to discover her there. "Anything wrong?" he asked.

"Yes," she said softly. "I need a kiss."

She found his face with her lips and kissed him.

"What are you thinking?" he asked, his words soft against her lips.

"About how much I love you," Rosie whispered. "Can love happen that fast?"

Del didn't answer. He showed her how quickly it could happen.

• • •

Pushing aside the broad flat rock, Del lifted the first of over a dozen rolled up, leather bound journals tied with leather thongs. A startled scorpion dropped out, causing him to fling the journal away and rear back. He felt like a fool, but that was all right. He didn't care. He was a happy fool.

Standing nearby, Rosie chuckled. "Be careful," she said.

"There's probably more."

The scorpion moved away with a disgruntled twitch of its insolently turned up tail.

And there were, indeed, several more scorpions, but eventually Del retrieved all the journals as well as the artifacts he had hidden there. He felt proud that he had saved Abner Saladay's research from Wesley Morris and his men. The ruins themselves would remain exposed to wind and weather and the curious who would surely come now, but the important initial observations Abner Saladay had made would endure.

Back in the house, Rosie made coffee. She had cornbread baking in the bake kettle in front of the fireplace. It was best coffee Del had ever tasted. He loaded it with sugar. It was a sweet delicious morning, and he was as happy as he could ever remember.

"I don't know, though," he said, munching the fresh cornbread. "I kind of miss the hard, dry stuff."

She ruffled his hair. He circled her waist and pulled her close for a kiss.

"We'll look for Old Belle and Faithful later," he said, accepting a plate filled with eggs and more coffee. "They can't have gone far," he said over a mouthful. "They'll need water by now."

"Unless Wesley Morris took them."

"Then we'll get him for horse stealing."

Rosie made a small smile. They both feared they weren't finished with Wesley Morris. Not yet.

Del finished his meal and watched Rosie finish hers. Her soft brown hair hung free, making her look girlish. He could smell her hair when she leaned close. There was a hollowness to her cheeks and a slight tremor of fatigue still to her small gravel-scuffed hand, but in time she would fill out, he thought. In time she would be rested. They were free now to find a new life together. It felt as natural as breathing.

"Ready?" he asked.

She nodded. It was time to look through the journals.

Del knew Rosie wanted to look at them. He worried the memory of Abner would spoil their happy mood, but he didn't feel right keeping her from what Abner had spent his life doing. She needed one last look. She selected a journal, untied the thong, and unrolled it. The journals were thick with many pages. Each journal was filled from cover to cover, each page from top to bottom all the way across the paper. Some were battered and worn with age. Del watched her thoughtfully turning the pages, smoothing them flat, looking closely, reading slowly.

She glanced up. "I never did learn to read so well," she admitted, "in the orphans' home. Could you read some of this for me?"

Rain during the night left new specimens of arrowheads unearthed all around where I sit. I ponder who once lived and worked here...

Del read several pages of observations and lists of things Abner had detailed during that period. In the earliest journals, Abner's comments were confined solely to his work. Together Del and Rosie pored over the diagrams of the ruins. Rosie was able to understand diagrams best. She searched each new drawing for where she had been trapped in the night and the tunnel where she escaped. They never found a drawing that suited her memory.

"I don't think he ever found that place," she said, looking surprised that she had found something about the ruins after all that Abner had never known.

In later journals, Abner's notes became more philosophical. He questioned his time spent there. He wondered who would ever value his work. He feared his discovery would be ignored, or worse, destroyed. He had never asked for help because he had been too selfish to share the discovery. He began commenting on Rosie more frequently. He was concerned about her, about the sometimes blankness of her expression.

I climbed to the topmost floor of the ruins this day, Abner wrote, detailing the height, general temperature and look of the canyon as he sat for hours, observing. *I long to bring Rosie here, but she is afraid of this place. Something haunts my poor dear. I long to share this wonder with her, this serene place I have come to love more than my life. But I have given up trying to convince her to join me. She is lonely, poor dear. She has done so much to make my life simpler so that I might do this work and not starve. I surely have not been the husband she dreamed of. She cannot imagine the depth of my regret over that. I shall never be able to make it up to her. I have grown old and stubborn in my work. I have not written to John in so long I am certain he has long since forgotten I ever existed. I shouldn't wonder if all my old friends at the Society assume I died here long ago. And surely, I shall die one day very soon. My heart flutters like a bird. I do not speak of it to Rosie. I would not worry my dear Rosie for the world.*

Del realized Rosie's face had gone slack with emotion. Tears welled in her eyes.

"What is it?" he asked.

"Abner thought about me," she said in a small voice.

Del leaned close. He pushed aside a tendril of Rosie's long hair and searched her eyes when she turned to him and tried to smile away her surprise.

"Do you miss him?" he asked, afraid of what she might say.

"He was never here enough for me to get used to him, so I couldn't miss him, could I?" Rosie said. "It's hard to believe I lived so long like that, afraid to be alone, but I was alone all the time! For my whole life almost. I was alone in the orphans' home. I was alone in the mill. I traveled all the way here—it took nearly two weeks—and I was alone the whole time."

Del watched her.

"I was always alone here," she went on. "I was alone when Abner was sitting right where you're sitting now. We're all alone… in our thoughts, aren't we? All those years, I was always afraid. I thought I needed someone to help me and do for me and take care of me. I was like a child in my thoughts and feelings. I realized… all this time… I've been helping myself, doing for myself, taking care of myself. I'm going to be all right."

Del drew away a little. He felt uneasy. What was she trying to say? "You don't need me anymore," he said, thinking his job there was done.

A radiant smile spread across Rosie's pretty sunburned face. "No," she said, smiling. "I don't need you! But I want you very much, Mr. Grant. When we get to town, would you buy me a ring?"

With overwhelming delight, Del kissed her hard.

"But not at Milt Brummit's store," she said, sobering. But there was still mirth in her eyes.

"Of course, Mrs. Grant. Whatever you want."

Fourteen

The plaza was quiet at two o'clock in the afternoon. The cottonwoods hung limp in the heat. A woman with a dark shawl over her head knocked at the closed door of Brummit's General Store. It was locked. Proprietor Milt Brummit had disappeared weeks before. A notice had been nailed to the porch post: *For Sale.*

At the rumble of an approaching column of riders followed by a covered wagon and a freight wagon pulled by a six-horse team, a clerk in sleeve garters came out of the bank to gawk. Two drifters came out of the saloon to watch from the shade of the porch.

Wesley Morris emerged from the office of the local miners' association, chewing a sharp new toothpick. He watched the lead rider, a gentleman on the fine bay mare, bring his procession to a halt. Morris planted his feet apart as if getting ready to receive the strangers.

There were ten well-appointed riders following the lead rider in front of the covered wagon. A burly driver and a scowling guard with a shotgun rode the covered wagon's seat. The outfit looked newly purchased in Tucson. Two equally intimidating men drove the freight wagon. It was loaded to full capacity and covered with a tarp, lashed down tightly with plenty of new rope. Three more riders, armed with pistols and rifles, brought up the rear.

Wesley Morris looked as if he was trying to hide his rising curiosity, but even across the plaza, Rosie, who was standing in the shade of the hotel's entrance, could see the tight, uneasy squint to his nosy observation. She took a deep breath but her new corset restricted her breathing. She stepped out onto the hotel's porch for a better look.

Judge Craig lumbered out of the restaurant's doorway next to the courthouse. He bowed to the cook and her husband who trailed after him, all curious about the newcomers riding in. The judge stepped back into the shade to watch. Seeing Rosie, he touched the brim of his hat and beckoned to her to join him. He started toward the gentleman dismounting the bay mare.

Rosie called back through the doorway of the hotel, "Del, they're here! They're here!"

Lifting her heavy new skirt hem, Rosie trotted through the pressing afternoon heat to the tall slender gentleman who scanned the town with an alert and rapt expression of observation.

Judge Craig joined her, smiling broadly. "You're looking lovely, Mrs. Grant."

"Hello, Judge," she replied. "Thank you."

Spying her, the newly arrived gentleman swept off his hat. He had grey curling hair, and though he looked immeasurably overheated and uncomfortable, he broke into a congenial smile. "Mrs. Saladay? Is it you?"

"Mr. John Hurley?" Rosie called. "Welcome to Diablo Rock. I can't tell you how happy I am that you could come so far, and so soon. It's Mrs. Grant now, by the way."

"Of course. Forgive me. How do you do?" he asked with admiration. "I remember Abner writing about you. Years ago, it was. When I got your telegraph message—" He bowed over her hand. "My deepest condolences on your loss."

"My new husband sent you the telegraph messages, Mr. Hurley. This is Delmar Grant," Rosie put in, realizing too late that she was being rude to interrupt. She motioned for Del to join the greeting. "I married again… recently." She was suddenly too overheated and excited to breathe.

"No need to explain, my dear," Mr. Hurley said, grasping her hands. "We all do as we must. Mr. Grant? I am honored to meet you, sir. And this must be Judge Craig. An honor, sir. Might we get inside out of the sun? I am very nearly dead in this heat. How Abner survived it as long as he did, I shall never know." He shook hands with Del and the Judge. Del grinned as he watched Rosie's happy face.

Rosie resisted planting a kiss on the cheek of the gentleman she had just met. He had a commanding manner that made her feel so very secure. He signaled the riders following him to carry on. The driver of the covered wagon slapped the lines and continued around the plaza toward the road south out of town. The younger gentleman riding directly behind Mr. Hurley, and four of the riders behind him, dismounted and approached.

"My assistant, Harrison Kaye," Mr. Hurley said of the handsome, well-dressed young man. "Harry, this is our famous Mrs. Saladay—do forgive me, dear. Mrs. Grant. And her husband—"

Wesley Morris sauntered across the street, the toothpick between his lips jutting upward as if held between clenched teeth. Poor man, Rosie thought with an inward chuckle. He was feeling left out. Her stomach gave a nervous flutter.

"What have we here, Rosie?" Mr. Morris bellowed as Mr. Hurley attempted to introduce his assistant to the circuit judge.

Ignoring Morris's thoughtless interruption, Mr. Hurley spoke a few private words to the judge while shaking his hand. "I'll meet you then for dinner, sir," he said to the judge.

Judge Craig lumbered back toward the restaurant, a self-satisfied smirk folding his face into amused lines of contentment.

Mr. Morris didn't like being ignored by the judge, and he hated having to look up at the tall newcomer in his dusty but elegant suit with the satin-piped lapels and black silk string tie. He appraised the heavy gold watch chain across the gentleman's flat belly and the expensive pistol peeping discreetly from the opening of his coat front. Even Mr. Hurley's riding boots were of better cut and quality than Morris's knee boots.

Rosie realized Wesley Morris looked like a rustic fraud, a second-rate gambler with audacious ambitions.

At last Mr. Hurley turned to Morris, his eyes seemingly warm with confidence and gentility. He looked him over in the very same manner Morris always did when trying to intimidate people, but when Mr. Hurley did it, it was so genuinely superior, Rosie felt thrilled to observe the difference.

"This is Mr. Morris," Rosie found herself saying. Her heart began to drum ever faster. She hadn't anticipated a confrontation so soon after her savior's arrival.

Mr. Hurley clicked his heels in the dust and gave a formal bow. "At your service, sir."

Morris's smirk widened around his toothpick. "What can I do for you?" His tone suggested he thought Mr. Hurley would be easy prey.

"You, sir?" Mr. Hurley asked. "I do appreciate the offer of assistance, however, I don't believe you can do anything whatsoever for me. I have come to survey the astonishing discovery made by Mrs. Grant's late husband. Abner Saladay was a schoolmate of mine, many years ago. A dedicated man of science. A great loss to the Society."

Rosie watched annoyance tinge Morris's now wooden grin. "And what kind of society would miss that crazy old fool?"

Boldly, Rosie took hold of Mr. Hurley's arm. She tugged at him gently. "You must be tired after your ride from Tucson, Mr. Hurley. Please ask Mr. Kaye and the others to come in for some water." She was afraid Morris was going to offend him. She wished Wesley Morris would just disappear.

Mr. Hurley looked down at her with such kindness in his eyes. "The teamsters need to continue on to set up camp and take over for the soldiers who have done us such a service, protecting Abner's valley these past weeks. I have already thanked Colonel Wills for his generous assistance. Without the help of the army we might have been at a distinct disadvantage. Abner's land extends some distance—I saw a map Abner sent some years ago. And, I believe I know who this man is," he said, indicating Morris. "I am more than happy to explain to him anything he would like to know. Here and now."

"Please do," she said, feeling Del draw her back into the shade of the nearest cottonwood.

"Let's go back to the hotel, Rosie," Del said close to her ear. "I think he can handle Wesley Morris."

Mr. Hurley patted her hand. "Go ahead, my dear. I'll be along in a moment. I don't believe Mr. Morris fully understands the situation."

As Del pulled Rosie several more steps away, Mr. Hurley turned his full attention on Wesley Morris and his flaccid smirk.

"Myself, and my assistant, Mr. Kaye, and my fellow scientists, Mr. Grayson, Mr. Sorenson, Mr. Abbott, and Mr. Thorley are here on behalf of the Ashmore Society of Anthropological Study of New York. We're here to set up the Saladay Research Site. I believe you know of the location. I was told you were trying to buy the land for a mere one thousand dollars."

Wesley switched the toothpick to the other side of his mouth with his tongue. "Still am. Offer still stands, Rosie."

But Rosie could see his calculating eyes flickering with a trace of uncertainty.

"Let me make something perfectly clear to you, Mr. Morris," Mr. Hurley said. "The telegraph being such a wonderful instrument of swift communication, I know all about you, sir. I will say this only once—"

"Forgive me, Mr. Hurley. Let me tell him," Rosie interrupted.

Mr. Hurley smiled. "Of course."

"Abner's valley is not for sale, Mr. Morris," Rosie said.

"It never was. It never will be. It belongs to the Society that Mr. Hurley represents. It has always belonged to them. I just didn't know it. Abner never explained."

She watched Wesley Morris's expression deflate.

"Abner Saladay and myself," Mr. Hurley went on for her, "and our fellows contributed to shares in the land Abner bought here ten years ago. Mrs. Sa—Grant has very generously donated her portion back to the Society. For the time being, I am in charge of the site. I may stay only a few months, but the Society's presence here is expected to be permanent. Are there any further questions, sir?"

Rosie watched with particular delight as the toothpick in Wesley Morris' mouth drooped.

"Now, Mrs. Grant," Mr. Hurley said, turning toward her, his dismissal of Wesley Morris complete, "if I might have that drink of water you spoke of. When Mr. Kaye and I are rested, I would most certainly like to ride out with you and your husband to see Abner's discovery."

He extended his elbow for Rosie to take. Rosie grabbed Del's elbow, too, and the three of them walked casually across the plaza to the hotel.

Rosie relished leaving Wesley Morris standing in the sun.

"I remember," Mr. Hurley said, smiling down at her, "that first letter of Abner's when he told me he had convinced an eighteen-year-old girl to come all this way to marry him. There were no children, I believe. I am sorry. I'm sure you know what a great man Abner was. Our most promising graduate. My best friend. When he came west for the lung cure, we were certain he would come back to us after he was well again. Until your telegraph message, Mr. Grant, I had no idea Abner had survived, nor the scope of

Abner's work. I missed him, but now I understand why he stayed here so long."

He turned to include Del in his smile.

"I owe you a debt of thanks for riding all the way to the fort to telegraph me of Abner's death," he went on, "and for the time you took to explain this. I would not have understood the urgency, otherwise. A marvelous instrument, the telegraph."

Del just grinned. "It was Rosie's idea to donate her share. When we read about the Society in Abner's journals, she knew immediately what to do."

"Ah, the journals. They're in a safe place, I hope."

"In the bank's safe."

"Excellent, but you both understand that the Society *must* reimburse you for the work you did on behalf of Abner's land. We are prepared to be most generous. Tell me, now, what are your plans?"

They stepped into the shade of the hotel's porch.

• • •

The valley looked different to Rosie. The house was still there but now it was surrounded by several canvas field tents, each with side panels rolled up to admit a cooling breeze. The footpath to the handprint entrance was well traveled now. There was a lean-to there as well. An armed guard spent his time there, making sure only the scientists came and went from the box canyon.

Mr. Hurley was Rosie's host now, showing her how the interior of the house had been changed, the roof shored up, more windows cut and framed in the adobe. A wooden trough had been built at the spring. The expedition's horses were stabled there under a newly constructed barn heaped with fodder.

"I hope you approve," he said as Rosie and Del accepted his invitation to look in at the box canyon. "You and Abner lived here... utterly remarkable!"

Rosie felt peculiar, seeing so much activity going on where once there had been only cacti, scorpions, and silence. She talked of things she remembered, but gradually she grew quiet. Both Del and Mr. Hurley noticed as they walked the distance to the handprint entrance. It was hot, and Rosie had a parasol to shade her face from the sun, but in a way, she felt as if she were visiting a grave. They had all been out to the cemetery to pay their respects at Abner's gravesite, but this was where he had died. This was where Rosie had dragged his body on the lean-to's poles. This was where it had all ended.

Inside the box canyon, Rosie was astonished to see all that had changed in the week since the Society's expedition arrived. There were markers of measurement everywhere. One of the scientists was sitting at a table under the shade of a canvas cover in nearly the same spot Abner once sat. The sight startled her. She looked to the place where she had found Abner's body and saw that someone had transplanted a prickly pear cactus near the spot, and watering it had produced a bud of a just-blooming cactus rose.

In that moment, Rosie felt Abner's love surrounding her, and it warmed her heart.

"Are you all right?" Del asked, seeing tears well in her eyes.

She nodded. "I'm ready to go if you are."

She didn't need to get any closer to the ruins. She wondered why, now, that Abner hadn't written to John Hurley sooner. Mr. Hurley had told her Abner never mentioned the ruins in his earliest letters. If it hadn't been for her, credit for the discovery of this place might have gone to someone else.

At the place where the handprint entrance opened into the box canyon, Rosie stood a moment, trying to remember who she had been that long ago day when Abner first brought her here.

When she turned to look up at Del, her heart felt very full.

"Are you sure you want to leave here?" Del asked. "We can stay if you want. I can find work here. Would you like that? Would you like to be close to the ruins and discover things?"

Del's eyes looked so gentle now. The darkness in them that had sometimes troubled her when they first met was gone. He had changed, too. He still wore his gun, but it was a formality now, not a necessity.

Looking back one more time, Rosie said her goodbyes to Abner and the ghosts who once whispered to her there. Then she took a firm hold of Del's hand and drew him into the shade of the looming boulders. They moved carefully through the stone passageway, and when they emerged in the valley, she paused to place her hand on the ancient handprint. She did not truly understand the part she had played in this place. She just knew that it was all right now to come away from it.

"Let's go," she said.

"All the way back to Virginia?" Del asked.

"Don't you want to? It sounded last night like you

wanted to. If your brother is there, we will see what happens. We can't know what we do sometimes, what it means, or where it will lead."

"Do you love me that much, Rosie?" Del asked.

"I love you," Rosie said.

"I think we should get married again."

She shook her head. "Our wedding was perfect. All I want is a ring."

Del's expression brightened, dazzling Rosie all over again with how wonderful his face was. His smile made her feel so happy. He was happy, too, and that was what mattered to her.

He reached into his vest pocket and plucked something small, round, and gold from the navy satin lining. He held up a ring with two fingers. She noted that his hand was shaking ever so slightly.

"I believe this is yours, Mrs. Grant."

Rosie's heart swelled with delight. "When did you get that?" she cried in surprise.

"Judge Craig brought it from Tucson yesterday. I nearly forgot about it."

She gave him a disbelieving smile. "You forgot. A likely story. I think Judge Craig likes you, Mr. Grant."

"I think he likes you, too, Mrs. Grant."

She grabbed his sleeve. She held out her left hand, fingers spread. Her hand was trembling ever so slightly, too. Del slipped the ring onto her fourth finger.

And then Del kissed her in front of the armed guard standing in the shaded heat of the lean-to near the handprint and the workers moving around the expedition's main campsite that encircled that ugly dirt-roofed house. Rosie closed her eyes and let herself get lost in Del's embrace. The hot sun beat down on her head, and the warm desert air pressed against her hands as she held the back of Del's strong neck.

There was no more darkness in Rosie's memory.

Only sunlight.

ANGEL

When her mother dies, fourteen-year-old Angel has no one to turn to but Dalt, a gruff-spoken mountain man with an unsettling leer and a dark past. Angel follows Dalt to the boomtowns of the Colorado territory, where she is thrust into the hardscrabble world of dancehalls, mining camps, and saloons.

From gold mines to gambling palaces, *Angel* tells the story of a girl navigating her way through life, as an orphan, a pioneer, and ultimately a miner's wife and respected madam…a story bound up with the tale of the one man in all the West who dared to love her.

AUTUMN BLAZE

Firemaker is a wild, golden-haired beauty who was taken from her home as a baby and raised by a Comanche tribe. Carter Machesney is the handsome Texas Ranger charged with finding her, and reacquainting her with the life she never really knew.

Though they speak in different tongues, the instant flare of passion between Firemaker and Carter is a language both can speak, and their love is one that bridges both worlds.

HURRICANE SWEEP

Hurricane Sweep spans three generations of women—three generations of strife, heartbreak, and determination.

Florie is a delicate Southern belle who must flee north to escape her family's cruelty, only to endure the torment of both harsh winters and a sadistic husband. Loraine, Florie's beautiful and impulsive daughter, bares her body to the wrong man, yet hides her heart from the right one. And Jolie, Florie's pampered granddaughter, finds herself in the center of the whirlwind of her family's secrets.

Each woman is caught in a bitter struggle between power and pride, searching for a love great enough to obliterate generations of buried dreams and broken hearts.

KISS OF GOLD

From England to an isolated Colorado mining town, Daisie Browning yearns to find her lost father—the last thing she expects to find is love. Until, stranded, robbed, and beset by swindlers, she reluctantly accepts the help of the handsome and rakish Tyler Reede, all the while resisting his advances.

But soon Daisie finds herself drawn to Tyler, and she'll discover that almost everything she's been looking for can be found in his passionate embrace.

SNOWS OF CRAGGMOOR

When Merri Glenden's aunt died, she took many deep, dark secrets to the grave. But the one thing Aunt Coral couldn't keep hidden was the existence of Merri's living relatives, including a cousin who shares Merri's name. Determined to connect with a family she never knew but has always craved, Merri travels to Colorado to seek out her kin.

Upon her arrival at the foreboding Craggmoor—the

mansion built by her mining tycoon great-grandfather—Merri finds herself surrounded by antagonistic strangers rather than the welcoming relations she'd hoped for.

Soon she discovers there is no one in the old house whom she can trust...no one but the handsome Garth Favor, who vows to help her unveil her family's secrets once and for all, no matter the cost.

SUMMERSEA

Betz Witherspoon isn't looking forward to the long, hot summer ahead. Stuck at a high-class resort with her feisty young charge, Betz only decides enduring her precocious heiress's mischief might be worth it when she meets the handsome and mysterious Adam Teague.

Stealing away to the resort's most secluded spots, the summer's heat pales against the blaze of passion between Betz and Adam. But Betz finds her scorching romance beginning to fizzle as puzzling events threaten the future of her charge. To survive the season, Betz will have to trust the enigmatic Adam...and her own heart.

SWEET WHISPERS

Seeking a new start, Sadie Evans settles in Warren Bluffs with hopes of leaving her past behind. She finds her fresh start in the small town, in her new home and new job, but also in the safe and passionate embrace of handsome deputy sheriff, Jim Warren.

But just when it seems as if Sadie's wish for a new life has been granted, secrets she meant to keep buried forever return to haunt her. Once again, she's scorned by the very town she has come to love—so Sadie must pin her hopes on Jim's Warren's heart turning out to be the only home she'll ever need.

TIMBERHILL

When Carolyn Adams Clure returns to her family estate, Timberhill, she's there to face her nightmares, solve the mystery of her parents' dark past, and clear her father's name once and for all. Almost upon arrival, however, she is swept up into a maelstrom of fear, intrigue, and, most alarmingly, love.

In a horrifying but intriguing development for Carolyn, cult-like events begin to unfold in her midst and, before long, she finds both her life and her heart at stake.

VANITY BLADE

Orphan daughter of a saloon singer, vivacious Mary Lousie Mackenzie grows up to be a famous singer herself, the beautiful gambling queen known as Vanity Blade. Leaving her home in Mississippi, Vanity travels a wayward path to Sacramento, where she rules her own gambling boat. Gamblers and con men barter in high stakes around her, but Vanity's heart remains back east, with her once carefree life and former love, Trance Holloway, a preacher's son.

Trying to reclaim a happiness she'd left behind long ago, Vanity returns to Mississippi to discover—and fight for—the love she thought she'd lost forever.